THE K.P. RANCH

Disaster struck the K.P. Ranch when rustlers stole two hundred head of cattle and kidnapped Curly Raine, the boss's younger son. When Curly's brother, Jim, and Rabby Buckthorne, the senior wrangler, set out on the vengeance trail, they discovered Curly's body hanging from a tree. A plugged peso was lying on the ground nearby — the trademark of Ben Jagar, the notorious half-breed outlaw. Then Rabby and Jim were captured by Jagar's ally, Pablo Ramiez, and death seemed inevitable . . .

RICK RICHARDS

THE
K.P. RANCH

Complete and Unabridged

LINFORD
Leicester

First hardcover edition published in Great Britain
in 2003 by Robert Hale Limited, London

Originally published in paperback as
Gunsmoke on the Border by Vern Hanson

First Linford Edition
published 2004
by arrangement with
Robert Hale Limited, London

Richards, Rick, *1920 – 2001*
   The K.P. Ranch.—Large print ed.—
   Linford western library
   1. Western stories
   2. Large type books
   I. Title II. Hanson, Vern. Gunsmoke on the border
   823.9′14 [F]
   ISBN 1–84395–580–6

Published by
F. A. Thorpe (Publishing)
Anstey, Leicestershire

Set by Words & Graphics Ltd.
Anstey, Leicestershire
Printed and bound in Great Britain by
T. J. International Ltd., Padstow, Cornwall
This book is printed on acid-free paper

1

Two hundred head of cattle were missing and that was a lot of beef to a small spread like the KP. It was as nothing though against the disappearance of Curly Raine, for Curly was the boss's younger son.

The night-riders came in one by one. They brought in two dead but Curly was not one of them. It had been a particularly dark night and they had been taken completely by surprise. Four horses had been killed. Men could do nothing on foot. They had fired at dark horsemen like speeding phantoms who vanished into the blackness with the surging cattle.

A bunch of men set out in the early morning to pick up the trail, to try and find Curly. They left behind a smaller bunch, digging graves, burying the dead.

Maybe another grave would be needed. Curly had got separated from the other boys and they hadn't seen hide nor hair of him when the raiders came and started the stampede. Curly could have been in the path of that mass of crazy, tumbling beef.

A lot of stuff still grazed, spread out all over the range. They had no time to round them up, and at first they figured there were more than two hundred or so missing . . .

They had to find Curly.

Seventeen, he was a popular young cuss. Still something mighty puppyish about him. Still the KP mascot the way he had been soon as he was born. His Ma died bringing him into the world.

There was another boy — he was two then — but he was different. Right from the first squall it had been evident that Jim had a mind of his own; he didn't aim to be anybody's mascot.

And now Jim led the bunch of men who went searching for his brother on the morning after the raid. Both brothers had had corn-silk hair and Curly's was still that way, wiry too, hence his nickname. But Jim's had darkened. It was dark brown, except at the front where the sun had bleached it. Jim was going on twenty now but he looked older. Tall, lean, with a narrow face and hot eyes and a mouth that was older and sterner than his years. Since his Pa had been laid up with arthritis Jim had taken over the running of the ranch.

Some of the men had objected to the whipper-snapper. Why, they could remember him in diapers! But he had proved himself, although in some cases he had had to use his fists to do it. He was handy with a gun too, a natural-born coiled spring with the striking speed of a sidewinder. But his speed hadn't been needed, except in a few friendly bottle-shooting contests back of the bunkhouse, and now the men accepted him and followed him.

Him and Rabby.

Rabby was senior wrangler at the KP.

He could have been called foreman maybe before Jim took over, except that Rabby never expected to be called anything. The men did what he told them because he was the best damned cattleman they knew and a wonder with horses too. It was said that Rabby loved horses more than he did men. And there were certainly times when he acted that way. But never with the two sons of his boss and old friend, Caleb Raine.

Caleb was a good man but not a tender one. He was a hard man of business. So it was Rabby who had virtually brought up the two boys and they loved him as much as they loved their father; maybe more so. He had always seemed old to them and now he was toothless and bent and bald. Nobody knew how old he really was but he still had more stamina than many of the young ones.

He rode beside Jim now, his old eyes sharp and anxious. As well as the best cattleman he was the best tracker in the territory too.

The course of the stampede was easy to follow. But Rabby was looking for signs of Curly and that was going to be harder. They ranged from side to side, covering a wide area. There was no chance of them catching up with the rustlers now, they had too big a start. Right now it was important to find Curly.

They came to a point where Rabby figured the cattle had run themselves out and slowed down. After that all the rustlers had had to do was haze them along to the buyer they had fixed, the running irons, or whatever hidey-hole they had for keeping rustled stock.

Dusk was falling when Rabby spotted something. Another fifteen minutes or so and he would probably have missed it altogether.

It was a red spotted cloth and everybody identified it as Curly's 'kerchief. It was in good condition except for a few mud-spots; it hadn't been trampled or anything like that.

The bunch went on, more cautiously now. The night closed in around them, another black one.

One of the night-riders whose horse had been shot from under him during the raid claimed to have seen the leader of the rustlers last night. A big man with a wide-brimmed sombrero and a mis-shapen shoulder. The description fitted the half-breed, Ben Jagar. There had been rumours that he was back in the territory.

Yeah, remarked Rabby, as they rode on now, maybe the night-rider had been right too. Up ahead was the range of God-forsaken rocky hills called the Crackerjacks, beyond them the scrublands and desert; these had been Ben Jagar's happy hunting grounds in the old days before the territory got too hot for him and he took his depredations elsewhere.

Rabby shut up then and did not speak the rest of his thoughts aloud. But he kept on thinking. Caleb Raine and Rabby and some of the older hands, still here now, had been the reason for Ben's flight. Old Caleb had been the fightingest man in those days! But now he was crippled with arthritis and maybe Ben had heard about this. And Rabby was older than ever, maybe already dead, Ben would figure. Maybe he had returned to get his own back, and line his pockets at the same time. The big black-hearted coyote had always been one with an eye for the main chance!

* * *

They found Curly on the edge of the Crackerjacks. His body hung from the bough of a cottonwood and spun gently with the wind.

Jim Raine lowered his brother gently to the ground as Rabby cut the rope. Jim sobbed but not for long. And when he rose he said:

'Take Curly back to the ranch. I'm going on.'

There was silence for a moment.

Then one of the men stepped forward uncertainly and said, 'I found this.'

It was Rabby who took it. It was a plugged peso. Ben Jagar's trade mark!

When Ben killed a man, beat him to the draw, it was his practice to toss a plugged peso beside the body. There had been a legend that Ben shot the hole in the peso himself. A fairy-tale, Rabby had always said. A heavy slug made a mess of a coin; these pesos were plugged too neatly, they were the kind of things that fancy-dressing Mexes had stitched to their chaps to prove how rich they were. Ben Jagar was half-Mex. He had no penchant for fancy dressing, except for that wide-brimmed sombrero. But he obviously liked fancy gestures.

Curly Raine had not been beaten to the draw. He had not been shot at all, just hanged like a dog. Ben had deviated from his usual procedure. Evidently he had wanted to be sure that Caleb Raine knew who was responsible for the execution of his youngest son. Probably Ben had a small stock of plugged pesos (he didn't kill a man every day, he didn't have a gunfight every day). And this to him must have seemed a special occasion well worth the expenditure of a peso.

Where did he get the things, wondered Rabby. From some Mex tailor probably . . . In his grief the old man's mind was wandering. He pulled himself up, hardened himself. He dropped the peso into the pocket of his vest and looked at Jim Raine in the darkness.

'I'm comin' with you,' he said.

They looked at each other in the darkness, not seeing each other but knowing each other. Jim inclined his head. He did not have to say anything. He turned to the boys.

'Rest of you go back. Take Curly. Grover, you're in charge in the absence o' Rabby an' me.'

'All right, Jim.' Grover Williams was a dour cuss but a good cattleman. The boys respected him and would do what he said.

Jim mounted his horse, turned it about. Rabby followed him. Nothing more was said. No goodbyes were called. The boys watched the two men until the darkness swallowed them up. Then the body of Curly was placed gently over the front of Grover's saddle and they went back the way they had come.

2

Jim and Rabby knew they were taking their lives in their hands. They were in Ben Jagar's own territory now. Although the half-breed outlaw had been away from it for so long there was no doubt that it would still be, to him, his own backyard.

Luckily, however, Rabby knew this territory well himself. He had lived near it for the major part of his life. There had been rumours, long forgotten now (Jim had been too young to hear them) that, in his youth, Rabby had lived in the Crackerjacks for years, hiding from the law that wanted him for something.

The two men rode in silence for a while. The one mourned an only brother who had been very close to him. The other, who had no real kith or kin, mourned a lad who had been like a son to him. Rabby had taught Curly to ride, to rope, to shoot, to read sign . . . He had taught Jim the same things too, but Jim had had a natural aptitude for these things anyway: already, for instance, he was the fastest gun on the KP. But Curly had lacked Jim's powers of concentration, he had been more slap-happy and less deadly. Rabby loved Jim like a son too, but Jim had never had to lean on him the way Curly had sometimes: the elder son, though barely twenty yet, was more than a match for his crotchety old Pa or anybody else. Erect in the saddle now, the boy was like the spectre of Old Man Vengeance himself: glancing at him there beside him in the darkness Rabby felt suddenly very old and inadequate.

He said: 'I know a box canyon where Ben might lay the cattle up to rest. He surely ain't gonna drive 'em right on through the badlands. Even if he means to try an' drive 'em across — if he's got a buyer the other side — he's gotta feed an' water 'em first or they'll never last. Even if you an' me ride our hardest we'll never get to this yere canyon before daybreak. We've come a long piece an' the hosses are tired. I know a little draw up ahead where we can hide a fire if we want one. I vote we rest a while.'

Jim remained silent, as if he was thinking things out. 'We can't bring Curly back now,' went on Rabby. 'There's no knowing how many men Ben has got. We ain't gotta give him a chance to bushwhack us, finish us before we've hardly got started . . . '

'You don't have to preach strategy to me you gabby old goat,' said Jim suddenly.

His voice was curt, humourless. Rabby was hurt. He was not sure what strategy meant, but that did not make the lash any less sharp.

'Lead me to this draw o' yourn.'

'All right, Jim.' Rabby realized suddenly that Jim was torn with grief for his brother and was fighting it. Like his Pa he had the appearance of fighting something all the time, if only inside of him. If he had not had a sense of humour too, something his Pa sadly lacked, he would have been a real mean one. As it was he was just dangerous. *A mighty dangerous young hellion*. Rabby decided to leave him be for a while. He led the way to the draw and they dismounted, neither of them speaking. They lit a small fire and brewed coffee and hotted up some beans. Then, after a quick supper, they doused the fire and separated into the shadows to lie down. They kept their guns by their hands. They did not aim to be bush-whacked while they slept.

Dawn was breaking when Rabby awoke and crawled over to Jim. The young man was still asleep but he looked as if he had had a struggle to attain slumber in the first place. His anguish of mind was written in the lines of his lean hard young-old face. Rabby let him sleep. He lit a fire, investigated the warbags and set about fixing some breakfast. It was lucky he had insisted that the men carry chow with them in case the trail was long. Even so, if Jim and he had to go into the badlands, there would be little enough for them and they would have to tighten their belts.

People had said that Ben Jagar had Apache blood in him, as well as the Lord knew what else. Maybe that was why — and Rabby remembered this from the old days — he seemed to be able to go such a long time without water. He always seemed to pick breeds and Indians and desert men to ride with him too.

Caleb Raine and Rabby had driven Ben Jagar out across the badlands in the first place. There had been rumours that he had been raising hell in Mexico since then. But he had come back out of the desert, out of the years. He had pounced treacherously, stinging like a scorpion and with fatal venom. This time there must be no let-up until he was crushed completely. Rabby had an idea it was going to be a long and horrible trail — unless Ben was already waiting round the nearest corner with another ready hang-noose — and he hoped young Jim would be here to see the end of it even if he wasn't. It had been a long life full of hell-raising and happiness and if Rabby could take Ben Jagar with him when he went, he figured he would die happy . . .

Jim stirred, moaned a little. Then he opened his eyes and sniffed the air.

'H-mm, bacon. Why didn't you wake me, you ol' goat?'

He sounded more affable this morning. But there was still that brooding sadness in his eyes, that savagery in the curl of his lips.

He joined the oldster, who said: 'I'm trying to avoid smoke. Ben might have a lookout on a high point someplace.'

But soon the breakfast was ready for eating, the hot thick coffee for drinking. They were able to douse the fire. They covered it over too, so that everything was cold. They didn't want anybody making a detour and picking up their trail.

Afterwards they rode on. Warily now, taking advantage of all the cover they could. Luckily there was plenty of it in this tortuous country. They were climbing most of the time. They kept pretty close to the cattle trail, though not near enough to be in danger of walking straight into a drygulch party. The cattle were having a rough passage. Like Rabby had said, Ben would have to rest them unless he wanted to kill them all off.

'He'll be expecting to be followed,' said Rabby. 'I got me an idee.'

He led the way again, leaving the trail they had followed. After a while the going was so rough that they had to dismount and lead their horses. Then finally they left them altogether, tethering them. And, as things turned out, it was a good thing they did.

★ ★ ★

The blue haze of the morning was dispelled. The sun beat down. There

17

was hard going for the two men and they sweated profusely.

'Surely there's an easier way than this one?' hissed Jim.

'There is,' said Rabby. 'But it's overlooked all the way round. If anybody's watching we'd be sitting ducks.'

They were climbing up to a craggy peak, larger than the hills around it, which was shaped roughly like a top hat. As Rabby had remarked earlier, however, it wasn't near as flat on the top as it looked from the distance. It would, though, give them a birds' eye view of the surrounding countryside and perhaps be the means of saving them from walking plumb into an ambush.

On the other hand Ben might already have a lookout up there. That was why Rabby had elected they leave the trail when they did and come by this tough and circuitous route, using shanks' pony only on the last spell.

Once more, though, Rabby proved to be right. And Jim half-admitted this when he inclined his head and hissed: 'Did you hear that cough? There's somebody up there already.'

'I thought I heard somethin'. If there is anybody up there, he certainly won't expect us to come this way. This is strictly for goats.'

After this they thought it best to be silent. They spread out.

They spotted the lookout. He sat with his back against a boulder. He was smoking, his rifle propped between his knees. He was facing away from the two men. Had he seen them earlier down there on the range? wondered Jim. Maybe he had only just arrived. Jim made a motion for Rabby to halt and the oldster did so. This last part was a young man's job, and who better to do it than Jim?

Jim rose, moved swiftly. But his high-heeled riding boots had not been made for such footwork over such ground. Pebbles rattled. The lookout whirled, scrambled to his feet, grabbing his rifle.

Rabby's gun was out. But it was not needed. Jim leapt. The guard went down with Jim on top of him. The rifle clattered on the rocks. There was the sound of bone striking flesh twice. The lookout lay still.

Jim rose, dusting himself off. 'Get down,' hissed Rabby, joining him. 'Mebbe this skunk ain't the only one.'

They got down in the cover of the boulder beside the unconscious lookout. Jim relieved the man of his gun and grabbed the rifle too. They crouched. Peering. Listening. Waiting. Nothing moved except a buzzard wheeling sluggishly high in the yellow sky. They heard nothing.

The lookout began to stir and moan. Jim bent over him, the man's own gun in his fist.

The man opened his eyes, began to raise himself.

'Stay right where you are,' said Jim.

The man saw the gun and froze.

'Where's Ben Jagar?'

'I don't know.'

The young man bent nearer. He pressed the cold muzzle of the gun to the lookout's temple. 'I haven't any time to waste. Either you tell me where Ben Jagar is or I press this trigger.'

The lookout gazed up into his captor's eyes and what he saw there made him shudder. This young man would do just as he said.

'He's in the box canyon with the boys and the cattle. But they'll be moving again soon.'

'All right. Get up.'

The man did as he was told. He looked deathly scared now wondering what was going to happen to him. In this lean young hellion with the levelled gun he saw a killer with no more feeling than a rattlesnake. He was a sneaky sidewinder himself, a murderer as were all Ben's boys; Ben picked them well. But the lookout did not think of this now.

'Where's your horse?'

'Down the back there.'

'All right, let's go down there.'

Some time later the three men, mounted, were on their way. The lookout was in the lead and Jim still had the gun pointed at the man's spine. The craven lookout had done some more talking. Yes, it was Ben Jagar who had given the order for Curly Raine to be strung up. Ben had said that he owed the boy's father plenty. Jim introduced himself as Curly's brother. The lookout was to lead Jim and Rabby to the box canyon. Although Rabby already knew where this was, Jim figured that they might be able to use the lookout to trick the outlaws in some way. The man knew that if he tried anything funny, young Raine would shoot him down like a dog, would probably be glad to do it as a little initial payment to avenge his brother's terrible death. The lookout remembered how the boy had kicked before dying, how Ben Jagar had laughed. The lookout was scared of Ben — the man was loco — but right now he was a damn sight more scared of the hot-eyed young killer at his back.

They paused once, thinking they heard something. But the wind had got up and it could have been only this they heard. There was a sudden change in the weather. Change often came like this in the hills. Dark thunderclouds obscured the sun and the wind played devilishly among the cracks and crannies.

They paused again, knowing that around the next bluff lay the entrance to the box canyon. There was a strange silence, none of the sounds of grazing cattle that they had expected.

Jim said: 'If you've steered us wrong . . . ' He left his sentence unfinished.

The outlaw bleated: 'I told you the truth. They've probably gone. That noise we heard a while back was probably the sound of the cattle moving out. I was to catch the boys up later . . . '

'So you know where they're making for?'

'Yes.' Having committed himself this far, the man couldn't very well say anything else.

'All right, go ahead. Take it easy.'

The lookout went around the corner of the bluff.

Up ahead a voice yelled: 'That you, Rube?'

Desperately, the man kneed his horse forward. 'Don't shoot! Yeh, it's me.'

Rabby and Jim turned the corner, guns at the ready. A man was rising from a cluster of rocks at the side of the canyon's mouth. He saw the two strangers and fired. But it was the luckless Rube who caught the slug. It knocked him clean out of his saddle.

Jim had a clearer view than Rabby, who was a little in the rear. Jim started shooting. He fanned the hammer of his gun, sending a stream of lead at the sniper before he had a chance to squeeze the trigger again. The man screamed once and disappeared from sight.

Rube was dead. So was the other

man. There was nobody else. Signs plainly indicative of the fact that the cattle, and Jagar's band with them, had indeed moved out.

'Ben don't take any chances, does he?' said Rabby. 'Another rear-guard.'

Standing over the second body, Jim cursed.

'I wish I had asked that damned Rube where the gang was going before we sent him around that corner.'

'Can't be helped,' said Rabby. 'We'll just have to follow the trail again that's all.'

3

They stopped at the edge of the badlands. A desert of short scrub and twisted mesquite and cactus stretched away in front of them under a grey lowering sky. Although the sun was hidden, the heat was oppressive. Away ahead the scrublands were hidden by a grey haze. Rabby said if it wasn't for this they might have been able to see the herd.

'It's a good job we can't in a way or, looking back, Ben and his boys might be able to spot us too, when we start to cross. If we were caught by them out there we wouldn't stand an earthly chance. On top o' that Ben might send scouts back — he's as cunning as an Injun. We won't have to push too hard an' we'll have to keep our eyes peeled.'

They had replenished their canteen at a spring Rabby knew of among the

26

rocks. It was surprising the things Rabby did know about this owl-hoot territory. Anyway, this was the last water they would be able to get until they got to the other side of the badlands and into Mexico.

They pushed on. The melancholy terrain seemed to close in around them as the light got even worse. The wind began to howl and soon they were in the centre of a minor dust storm. They pulled their kerchiefs up to cover their mouths.

Rabby cussed into his gag. If this kept up the tracks would be obliterated. Ben Jagar, who knew this territory like his own back-yard (hell, it was his own back-yard) was liable to veer off in any direction.

The dust storm ceased as suddenly as it had begun. The wind lessened. Fat drops of rain plummeted from a steely-grey sky. Rabby, taking his muffler from his mouth, groaned aloud. He rode bent almost double in the saddle, peering at the ground most of the time. Rain continued to threaten. The fat drops fell and were swallowed up by the dust.

'It's like I thought,' said Rabby.

Then, as Jim turned enquiringly towards him: 'The herd that's bein' driven now is a helluva lot bigger than the one Ben took from us. He must've had a lot more rustled beef in the box canyon just waiting to be driven. Now he's taking his whole bunch to a market in Mexico.'

The rain came down with sudden fury, almost drowning Rabby's last words.

He yelled another sentence or so but Jim couldn't hear a thing. The dust could not hold this watery fury and pretty soon the ground was soggy, networked with rivulets.

Rabby moved his horse closer so they were side by side. He bellowed: 'At least there's no need to go thirsty now. I bet Ben and his rustled cattle are glad o' this.'

Jim did not say anything. There was

nothing to say. He did not know as much about this territory as Rabby did, but he did know that here rain was a rarity. Wasn't this just their damnable luck? There would be no trail left after this, that was certain sure!

He had a slicker across his saddle. But the storm had come so suddenly, soaking him to the skin, that he didn't think there was any use in covering himself up now. The rain cooled him, loosened him up a bit. He had been like a caged tiger, prowling. Now he realized that, if it hadn't been for old Rabby, he might have run head-on into something by now. Then how would Curly be avenged? He tried to shut from his mind the vision of his brother's body at the end of the rope, spinning gently with the wind. He lifted his face up to the rain, let it beat on him, blinding him. He sucked the wetness into his mouth.

Rabby had not bothered to put his slicker on either. He figured it was time he had a bath. They pushed on against the fury of the storm and after about half an hour or so it abated. Finally it stopped altogether and the sun shone again. The haze had gone and the badlands stretched out before them for countless miles.

But there was no sign of a dust-cloud caused by cattle. Or anything moving at all. And the trail was totally obliterated. The ground drank, steaming; the stunted vegetation seemed a little brighter. But the two partners looked at each other glumly, wordlessly. Until Rabby said: 'Let's just keep ridin'.'

And Jim Raine did not have to say anything to this. He would keep riding to the end of the earth to catch the man who had murdered his brother.

* * *

They ate and drank a little as they rode. They tried hard to pick up the trail. They did not do so. But they had a stroke of luck in another way. As Rabby said afterwards, it was *their* turn; the devil had had all his own luck up to now. The devil being Ben Jagar.

The old prospector tried to avoid them, as well he might do in this lawless territory. But they had spotted him from miles away and they wanted him. Short of turning back he could not miss them and the old goat did not seem inclined to turn back.

When they rode up to him he had the drop on them with his shotgun. It was an ancient weapon but looked capable of blowing a hole as big as a door in any man. And the bewhiskered face above it was suspicious, choleric and uncompromising. The prospector spat a stream of baccy juice neatly between the wing-ears of his mule without batting an eyelash. The beast seemed to have gone to sleep, as did the other mule, pack-laden behind.

'What do yuh want?' demanded the ancient man.

'Nothing but information,' said Jim Raine.

'I didn't think an old friend like you

would ever threaten me with a sawn-off, Nevady,' said Rabby.

Jim turned and looked at his companion then back once more to the prospector.

The latter squinted suspiciously. He looked as if he was due to start blasting at any minute. Jim got ready to fling himself sideways from the saddle and get his gun out at the same time. If his head was not already blown off before he hit the ground. But suddenly, behind the grey matted whiskers, the ancient prospector's face lit up.

'Jumpin' Jehosophat. Young Rabby Buckthorne!' The whiskered oldster lowered his gun, kicked his mule. The animal moved sluggishly forward. The two men pumped each other's hands while Jim looked on with mingled emotions on his lean young face.

Finally Rabby had to curb the solitary old man's exuberance. They had no time to waste and there were questions to be asked. So Rabby asked them. And got good answers.

Yes, Nevada had seen a large herd of beef. And he had given it a wide berth. He had figured it was probably being driven by Ben Jagar and his hell's spawn and they were on their way to the ranch of that old demon, Pablo Ramiez, with whom Ben did most of his business.

'Are we on the right track?'

'Wal, yeh, almost.' Nevada turned, pointed. 'See that tall prickly pear out there — it's a helluva lot further away than it seems — it's a real giant?'

'Yes.'

'Make for that. An' when you get there look up ahead again an' you'll see a kind of a hump. It ain't what you might call a hill. Just a itty-bitty thing. But it's the only hump hereabout. A straight line from that hump leads you right to the edge of Pablo Ramiez's land. But watch your step — Pablo's hellions shoot first an' ask questions afterwards.' Nevada squinted at Rabby. 'You ain't turned lawman or somethin' have you, *amigo*?'

'Not exactly.'

'I never thought young Rabby Buck-thorne would turn lawman. Though they do say . . . '

'I'm working for the KP Ranch on the other side of the Crackerjacks,' put in Rabby. 'I told you that last time we met. Hell, I bin working there more years than I can remember. What's happened to your memory, you old mossy-horn?'

'Wal, Rabby, they do say that if a man lives to be as old as I am his memory starts skipping things an' going back to when he was a young sprig full of sap and devilment.'

Jim jerked his horse forward. 'Stop in at the ranch any time you're that way, Nevady.'

The old man's eyes were sharp in that mat of whiskers. He saw that this young hellion was raring to go. He said: 'Wal, I dunno what you're up to an' I got more sense than to ask. But I wish you luck any way. You'll need it if you aim to tangle with the Jagar and Ramiez bunches. An' it ain't just luck you need. You need a goshdurned army to back it up . . . C'mon gel.'

They watched him go and he turned once and raised his hand in salutation. They set their horses to a faster pace and not till they reached the outsize prickly pear that Nevada had pointed out to them did either of them speak. Then Jim said: 'He called you *young* Rabby Buckthorne.'

'Yeh, I allus told yuh I was just a chicken.'

'I'd almost forgotten you had such a fancy last name too. Buckthorne! Ain't that something?'

'I come from aristocratic stock,' grinned Rabby. They set off for Nevada's 'hump' which was now plain to see.

'I hope Nevady ain't steered us wrong.'

'Me too,' said Jim.

He did not look quite so tense. He had even cracked a joke; a good sign, Rabby reflected. The boy was not so liable to go off half-cocked now. Jim set his horse at a gallop and Rabby went after him.

They kept this up till they got to the hump and then Jim dismounted as Rabby caught up with him. The younker's eyes were not so hot and wild now in his stern face. But there was still that brooding sadness there and Rabby's heart went out to this boy who was like a son to him. Blood would flow before that brooding shadow could be dispelled.

Jim crawled to the top of the hump and looked out across the badlands. He called down, 'There's a film of dust out there but I can't see anything moving. The territory's a little more rugged out there.'

'We're getting near to the edge of the badlands,' grunted Rabby, joining him.

They kept watch for a bit but saw nothing moving except a couple of nosy buzzards up above. But even these carrion, seeing that the two men were still alive and kicking, finally flapped lopsidedly away, their derisive cries dying in the stillness.

There had been what seemed like a film of dust, perhaps the backwash of a herd, but now even that had gone. There was nothing. The two men got down. They sat in the shelter of the hump for a bit out of the sun. Then the shadows came after they had no more water and food and, by that time, they were on their way again. Rabby had called the edge of the badlands 'near' but there was no sign of them yet. Had Rabby misjudged? Jim wondered. But he did not voice his thoughts and, when Rabby suggested that they bivouac for the night, he complied.

This time they did not light a fire, knowing it would be seen for miles. They had nothing to cook or boil anyway; they just lay down.

They talked it over and decided to rise before daybreak and push on. They aimed to get into cover before broad day.

Jim did not sleep. He lay awake

gazing up into the dark sky, his hands behind his head. The sky was blank but his thoughts were not and he wished he could sleep. He told himself that he must have strength for what he had to do. But still he could not sleep.

The hours passed like ages broken only by the soughing of the wind and the occasional cry of a night bird. Finally he crawled across the ground and awakened Rabby. The oldster was alert instantly, his hand on his gun. He squinted up at Jim. Then he took out his ancient gold hunter watch, his proudest possession, and gazed at it.

'Yeh,' he said. 'It's time we were moving all right.'

They rode cautiously and soon moved on to a rock surface. 'This is it,' said Rabby and Jim realized the old man had been right after all. The night was so still that, despite their caution, their horses' hooves now made quite a clatter on the rock floor as the beasts picked their way around outcrops and slid on the uneven surface.

The night was hot and men and beasts, having been without water for some time, were parched. Already the men could smell grass. It was a strange phenomenon of this cruel and magical land that change was so sudden, aridity giving way to succulence, death to a bursting life. The horses smelled the moisture and the feed and despite the steadying hands on their reins, surged and scrambled, their heads forward-thrust. They awakened the echoes in the hot night.

Rabby reined in his mount, gentling the trembling beast with his hands, whispering soothing words into his quivering ear.

Jim followed suit, but looked back a little impatiently. Then Rabby said: 'I reckon we oughta muffle their hooves somehow,' and Jim realized that once more the oldster was right.

He said: 'I got some burlap strips in my warbag. I was gonna use 'em to make myself a new rifle sheath.'

'The rifle sheath can wait. They're

just what we need.'

Jim produced them. The two men got down. They wrapped the burlap strips around their horses' hooves, cutting some of the stuff into thinner strips for tying material. Soon they were ready to go again. And this time the beasts did not make half so much noise.

The rock terrain was now becoming broken up by vegetation of a far more succulent nature than they had passed out in the badlands proper. There was grass here and there too, in the crevices of the rocks. The men allowed their horses to stop and nibble a little before pushing them on again. And now the beasts, their thirst assuaged a little by the moist grass, seemed to understand the need for caution themselves and so went more gently.

The whole effort was spoiled, however, when one of the beasts whinnied. Almost at the same instant Rabby, who had eyes like a hawk, said: 'Light up ahead.'

The two men reined in. Now Jim saw

the light too. He agreed with Rabby that it was not made by a fire. More likely by the window of a small cabin or something like that.

'D'yuh think there are horses up there? This crittur seemed to think so.'

'Probably outside the cabin, or whatever it is,' said Rabby. 'Still some distance away yet though, so maybe we weren't heard. What do yuh think, Jim; shall we tether these critturs someplace an' creep up on foot?'

'Seems the best bet.'

'All right.'

They dismounted. They tethered the horses to a crimp of non-prickly cactus of a much stronger kind than that they had passed earlier. They went on on foot, spaced a little apart. Already their guns were in their hands.

The light got larger and brighter up ahead and soon they realized it was indeed the window of a cabin, probably a remote line-hut or something like that. There was no sound from up there. No horses moved or called.

The two men passed an outcrop of rock, one of the largest they had seen since they left the Crackerjack range behind. They both heard the noise but by then it was too late; even as they started to turn, the sibilant Mexican voice said: 'Stay steell. Drop your guns.'

They sensed the presence of more than one man. They let the guns fall. Their clatter on the rock surface was like a knell of doom. Was their quest for vengeance to be ended almost before it had been started? They were both savage with themselves. They had walked into a trap like two babes. The whinnying horse had been heard; and now they were caught not only on foot but almost literally with their pants down.

4

'You can turn around now, *señors*,' said the Mexican voice.

Quite an educated-sounding voice.

The two *señors* turned around and faced their captors and were not surprised to discover there were four of them. They all held guns. The talking one was a little in front of the other three, who looked pretty dumb anyway. This one was so obviously the talking one, the educated one. He was young and tall and handsome and beautifully dressed in a florid Mexican style. His gunbelt was chased with silver and his holster was low and fastened to his thigh by a whang-string. He looked as dangerous as a diamond-backed rattler and this despite the fact that, in the half-light, he was smiling suavely. He was like a rattler lying low and beautiful, coiled to strike.

The other three men were just peons, greaser cowboys. Dirty, villainous-looking, what little finery they had very much the worse for wear. But their guns were well-cared for and they held them steadily and looked more than ready to use them.

Dawn was breaking slowly. The sky was tinged with flecks of red, the colour of blood.

Jim Raine couldn't help feeling that they hadn't been very clever after all. Maybe they ought to have brought more men with them, even though it would have meant depleting the force at the KP, laying it open for further attack.

Rabby's and his teeth had been drawn and, in any case, they were outnumbered by two to one. There seemed little hope unless something happened. These four ginks were not peaceable. They had blood in their eyes. Maybe they had even been sent to look out for him and Rabby. When the two guards from back at the Crackerjacks had not turned up, Ben Jagar would have guessed that something had happened. It was more than probable that these four Mexes belonged to the rancho of Ben's ally, Pablo Ramiez, 'that old demon' as Nevada had called him.

Jim wished he still had his gun, even if it was holstered. He was fast with his gun. He figured that in a straight fight he stood a chance with any two of the scruffy peons, maybe all three of them. But the fancy boy was a different proposition altogether. He wore his gun like a professional, he handled it that way. He carried himself like a man who was proud of his prowess with a gun. These high-born Mexes were a proud people in many ways, Jim knew. Was this one proud enough to give the other man an even break?

These thoughts shot through Jim's mind in infinitesimal moments. He had no means of knowing what Rabby thought. Maybe Rabby's thoughts were very much the same as Jim's. Despite his lack of learning Rabby was a very intelligent old cuss. Jim could not have picked a better man to be his companion on this pilgrimage. He would not have picked another man had he had the choice of the best fighters in the West. And Rabby was one of these too. He could not have picked a better man to die with, Jim reflected sardonically.

The fancy boy had savoured his triumph to the full. Now he spoke again.

'Now you've had a look at us, *señors*, and know we mean business you can turn around again and walk towards the hut.'

They turned around. They heard one of the peons pick up their guns. 'March,' said the leader and they marched.

They heard the leader tell one of the peons to go back and fetch their horses and they heard him go. So now the odds were only three to two. But what good did that do them?

There were four horses under the

stunted cottonwood by the cabin. The cabin itself was just a one-roomed log building plastered with adobe mud. The usual line hut, containing a couple of crude bunks, a table, a small oil-burner for cooking purposes if the weather was unsuitable for a fire outside. A couple of chairs and some old packing cases for further seating accommodation if needed . . .

The place stank. The heat was trapped in here with the cooking smells and the stench of unwashed bodies. The fancy Mexican looked even more out of place here than did the two travel-stained Americans. But the two peons were in their element; and now their companion joined them, telling the chief that he had put the gringos' horses with the others beneath the cottonwood.

Rabby and Jim were sitting side by side on one of the bunks, wondering what was going to happen to them. The three peons kept their guns levelled but the chief had put his away in its beautiful holster.

'What are you going to do?' asked Jim. 'Shoot us like dogs?'

'You weell see,' said the chief. Now in the smouldering light of a hanging hurricane lantern he looked little older than Jim and probably wasn't.

'We might hang you,' he said conversationally, flashing his white smile in his dark handsome face. He turned his head. Dawn was filling the cabin and soon there would be no need for the lamp.

We did not even gauge our time properly, thought Jim bitterly. We should have been further on by this time. In fact, we planned to be at the rancho before dawn came. But he blamed himself more than Rabby. He had gone on half-cocked from the very start, so great had been the shock of his brother's terrible death. He wondered what his crippled father was doing and thinking now. What would he think when he learned his other son was dead, perhaps lynched too, as his younger one had been? If he ever learned; if Jim and Rabby were not considered, after the years had passed, to be yet more victims of Nature in the treacherous badlands . . .

'To be hanged in the flush of the dawn is a brave way to die,' said the Mexican chief.

'I don't think so,' said Rabby grinning toothlessly.

Even so, the oldster did not seem at all put out by the prospect.

'They only hang bushwhackers and horse-thieves and rustlers,' said Jim Raine. 'It is a shabby way for a man to die when he has committed no crime. What are we supposed to have done?'

'You were caught trespassing,' said the chief. 'It is my experience that trespassers are always either horse-thieves or rustlers.'

'Quit play-acting,' said Jim harshly. 'Admit that you were sent out to stop us and deal with us. To hang us and tell yourself that you're doing this because we are thieves an' deserve no better is just the excuse you will be giving yourself.' He glanced at Rabby and his lips curled. 'But I guess we couldn't really expect anything else from a cowardly greaser, huh; pardner?'

The astute Rabby saw what Jim was trying to do. 'I could've told you that in the first place, Jim,' he said. 'I'm a lot older than you an' I know these greasers. They're all alike, fancy clothes an' fancy talkin' or not. They're treacherous back-shooting skunks . . . '

The young Mexican's face flamed with demoniacal rage. It was that hated word 'greaser' that had done it! His lips drew back from his teeth and he started forward and slashed Rabby across the mouth with the back of his hand.

The force of the blow knocked Rabby back across the bunk. But when he straightened up he was still grinning with bleeding lips. 'See what I mean, Jim?' he said.

Jim glared at the young Mexican with a well-simulated look of rage and disgust. 'Yeh, I see what you mean,

Rabby. Trust a greaser to pick on an old man as well, instead of a young sprig like me who's about his own age . . . '

'Hell, I ain't old. I could take him with one hand tied behind my back. But, don't you worry, that yellow skunk ain't gonna give me the chance, not while he's got three of his stinking pardners to do his dirty work for him.'

The two pardners were playing with death and they knew it. And death held all the best cards. It was not true that all greasers were, as Rabby had said, 'backshooting skunks'. Many of the higher-born Mexicans of ancient Spanish lineage (and this character could be one of them — had Don Pablo Ramiez a son, wondered Jim) had an almost nonsensical conception of honour and chivalry and what a fighting man could and could not do. But they were also an unpredictable breed: there was nothing worse than a really bad greaser, whether high-born or not, except perhaps a blood-thirsty Apache.

This character was quite likely to slit

their throats out of hand and save the strain on a hemp rope after all. Right now he looked quite capable of doing just this. His face had gone pale beneath its swarthy tan. His eyes were calculating slits. His three cohorts stood by like hounds straining at the leash. They were just waiting for the word to turn this cabin into a blood-bath.

'Go on, get it over with,' said Jim Raine. 'Let the boys have their fun. Or maybe you'd like that fun yourself? Why don't you take out that fancy gun of yours an' shoot us down?'

'I think he's only got it for show,' said Rabby. 'I bet he cain't even shoot straight. I bet from where he's standing he cain't even hit me.'

Rabby was still grinning, Blood ran down his chin from his busted mouth and gave him a ghoulish appearance.

Jim said: 'You better turn your back or he's bound to miss you. You know what these greasers are. It scares them to shoot to a man's face, even if the man is unarmed.'

The young Mexican took out his gun. He was composed now, a real poker face.

'Call that a draw,' sneered Jim. 'We got an old Chinee cook back at the ranch who can draw faster than that.'

'Give me a Chinee 'fore a greaser any time,' said Rabby.

The young Mexican's expression did not change. He did not raise his gun, just elevated the muzzle a bit. The gun barked. Rabby gave a little hiss of pain. It was very unexpected. He clapped his hand to his ear. His fingers came away splotched with blood. The ear had been neatly nicked.

'He missed me,' carolled Rabby, deliberately misinterpreting the reason for the shot.

Jim turned and looked at him, then looked back at the Mexican, at the smoking gun in his hand. 'He meant to do that, don't you see, Rabby,' he said judiciously. 'He's tryin' to prove to us that he can shoot after all.'

'Oh.' Rabby kept his mouth open and

his eyes wide as if a great light had suddenly shone upon him. Then he began to wag his head slowly from side to side. 'Circus stuff,' he said. 'Anybody can pink a man when he's standing still. The test is can he stand up to another man with a gun an' both of 'em with their guns holstered . . . '

'No greaser can do that,' said Jim. 'Leastways not against an American.'

Jim began to move then. He moved slowly forward towards the fancy boy and his levelled gun, towards the four levelled guns. The three peons glanced at their chief in consternation. They wanted to shoot down this crazy young gringo but they could not do so unless their chief gave the word.

And the chief acted strangely. He even backed away a little. And he was smiling.

* * *

'You are fast with a gun mebbe, *señor*?' the chief said.

'Fair to middlin',' said Jim Raine.

'He's fast enough to take care of any damned greaser,' blustered Rabby Buckthorne.

'You theenk, old one?' said the chief silkily. He was really play-acting now, preening himself.

His followers were puzzled and uneasy. But his acting was not for them. They were peons: they were but as dogs. His acting was for these two hated Americans. He wanted them to know well who was their master before he killed them both. First the young one, and then the old one, and in the proper way too.

He hated Americans who looked down on his people, who had taken Texas from his people. His father had been killed by the Americans, so he owed them much. His father had been an honourable man and would want him to do it this way. He smiled to himself. It would be easy. Too easy. Was not he the fastest gun on the border? Maybe he could take them both together . . .

But no, that would be the gesture of a fool (the young one could be quite fast): he decided against it.

He said, 'Let us all go outside. Look, is it not a beautiful morning now on which to die?'

'The light's kinda bright,' said Rabby.

His young companion did not say anything. The chief put this down to fear. The young gringo was all wind. The chief hugged himself with silent glee.

So they went outside and the chief told one of his followers to give the young gringo his gun. The peon did what he was told: who was he to question the decisions of his betters? The young gringo holstered his gun and the chief followed suit and then he told his followers to put away their guns too. They did as they were told and the two youngest men faced each other and the peons watched and the old one stood a little separated from everybody else and he watched too.

It worked, thought Rabby. Jumping Jesophat, it worked! But could Jim take this young Mex? Jim was fast. But this young Mex looked fast too: he looked mighty sure of himself . . .

What are you, you old goat? Rabby asked himself savagely. What was that old saying about a faint heart? Not the one to do with the female sex. The other one. He couldn't remember it . . . Hadn't he any faith in his young pard? Why, he was the one who had taught the young hellion to shoot in the first place! Of course he had faith in him. Of course . . .

Jim remembered one thing Rabby had told him. He watched his opponent's eyes. Even the most professional gunfighter's eyes gave him away sometimes that small moment before he went for his gun.

But this Mex's face was expressionless, real poker type, and his eyes were like small black marbles with no look in them at all.

Jim knew he was up against a real

gunfighter. A man who had cold courage too. He *knew* he could beat Jim. And Jim, in his turn, knew that it was he and only he could be the victor. They were both young and arrogant and had nerves of steel. So it had to be decided.

It was soon over, that split moment between a man's living and a man's utter irrevocable death.

Who went for his gun first, who made that tiny movement that gave him away to the other one, precipitating the sound and the fury and the death? Nobody among the watchers could have answered this question as they were caught rigid in a moment of time as the fighters blurred in violent action.

The blatter of shots was hideous in the rocky stillness.

The Mexican's lean form caved in the middle. His eyes mirrored disbelief and terrible agony. His gun was in his hand still and he fired and the shot went wild and Jim Raine shot a second time. The heavy slug struck home higher up this time, spinning the man round. He dropped his gun in the dust. He corkscrewed. He fell in a heap like a gaudy crumpled doll. He lay still.

Jim whirled and Rabby dived. Jim's third shot knocked a peon flat, his gun only half out of its holster. Rabby scooped up the fallen gun, fired from a kneeling position. Another peon clawed at himself and went down. He had had a chance to fire at Jim but in his haste had missed completely. He did not have a second chance. He was as dead as his comrade. The third peon screamed. He threw his hands above his head and babbled for mercy in his own tongue.

Both men advanced on him. Rabby took his knife and gun. Jim jerked a thumb, indicating the body of the chief. 'Who was he?'

'Don Pablo's younger brother, *señor*. His only brother.'

'I had an only brother too,' said Jim tonelessly.

5

They buried the chief and his two cohorts beneath a pile of small rocks to protect them from the buzzards and coyotes. The chief, at least, had been a brave man, if a conceited and foolhardy one. He deserved the semblance of a civilized burial.

They tied the horses more firmly so they would not escape and return instinctively to the rancho, thus giving the game away. They let the living peon keep his horse and they mounted their own. They made the peon lead the way. He was to take them to the rancho. He was to be their slender bulwark, if need be. If he was a good greaser maybe he would live to a ripe old age after all and be able to tell his grandchildren of the battle he had just seen and the young gringo with lightning hands.

The country got more rocky as they went along. But there were increasingly larger patches of lush grass too. It seemed almost incredible that grass could be so lush here on the edge of the badlands. This was just another example of nature's strange phenomena, the benignity after the cruelty. They saw cattle here and there in twos and threes, doubtless strayed a little from the main herd. They saw no riders. The cattle looked plump and healthy stock. Jim roped a steer and they took a look at the brand. It was a sort of a window pattern with lots of little squares.

'Is this Pablo Ramiez's brand?' asked Jim.

'Yes, *señor*,' said the peon.

'Neat. You could pretty well blot out anybody's brand with that one without having to put in some clumsy work with a running iron.'

'It's bigger than the usual, too,' said Rabby. 'A real blotter. I wonder who this crittur originally belonged to. Still,

I guess Don Pablo has got a *few* cows of his own.'

'I guess KP cattle'll soon be salted in among this lot,' said Jim savagely.

'Well, if this is the way Ben Jagar is getting rid of his stolen beef it's certainly a sweet little set-up.'

They reached a small hill clustered with queer-shaped outcrops and rock formations. The sun was up now. Its rays rebounded from the rocks with piercing ferocity. Luckily, the men and horses had had themselves a drink and filled their bottles back in the cabin. Even so, it was mighty hot.

The peon indicated that they would come in sight of the ranch on the other side of the hill. But the hill was broken up in places and there was a quick way through, saving them the trouble of climbing or going round. The peon led the way.

The cleft was almost hidden by a fall of rock. Had the two Americans been alone they would surely have missed it. There was only room for riders to travel one abreast. Rabby followed the peon and Jim brought up the rear. Neither of the two KP men had their guns out now. They figured the Mexican was well and truly scared. What could he do anyway?

Pretty soon he showed them just what he could do!

He turned a corner quickly and urged his horse to a gallop. At first, as he passed out of sight, Rabby did not tumble to what he was up to. Then the sound of the galloping hooves echoed through the air and the man began to shout piercingly for help.

Jim cursed savagely, kicking his horse. The startled beast bounded forward, cannoned into its mate in front, almost unseating Rabby. Rabby's horse shot forward. The oldster, doing a mite of cussing himself now, was almost knocked off against the rock wall.

'Sorry,' mumbled Jim. He could not get by.

Rabby's horse turned the corner. Jim's horse followed suit. Their riders, perforce, had to go with them. It was a good job they were going in the right direction. There was no room to do anything else. There was an incline and a bottleneck. The peon had known this. Doubtless he and his horse had negotiated them so many times that they could have done them blindfold. There was another bend up ahead and the peon had gone round this and was already out of sight.

Rabby's horse slipped and lost his footing on the rocky slope. He could not fall over, there wasn't room, but he cannoned back into Jim's horse, thus getting his own back for the buffeting he had received from that beast a moment ago. But neither horses nor riders were very pleased about all this. They got up there at last. They turned the second corner. The cleft widened again but still there was no room for two abreast. And no sign of the fleeing peon, though they could still hear his yells. Rabby pushed on as fast as he could. The fuming Jim brought up the rear.

They broke out of the rocks at last and before them was a stretch of lush green rangeland and a large cluster of buildings in the heat-haze. Even in the distance Pablo Ramiez's place looked more like a fort than a ranch. Between it and them the fleeing peon was like a flapping turkey. More riders suddenly appeared, speeding towards the man.

'I guess we better make ourselves scarce,' said Rabby. 'We can't fight an army. After this I'll never say Mexicans are dumb,' he added disgustedly. 'That dirty-looking skunk must've had that planned all along.'

They turned their horses, went back through the cleft as fast as they could make it. This was the only way they knew. They certainly didn't want to waste time in climbing or making detours.

They reached the other side of the hill. But they could still hear sounds of pursuit, hooves striking rock, the sounds echoing and re-echoing.

They had a pretty good start but their horses were tired after the desert journey. And the pursuers knew the country. 'Let's take it this way,' said Jim. 'Mebbe we can hole up someplace.'

But he just led them into another bunch of men driving strays.

Rabby's horse was shot from under him and the oldster lay stunned. Jim was surrounded by a bristling ring of guns. Not being completely loco, he allowed himself to be disarmed.

★　★　★

It was night again. Pablo Ramiez was alone with his grief for his young brother, Ramon. His only brother, he who had so many sisters. The child of his parents' old age, the child that, when they died, he had promised to look after always. Ramon had been a wild one, a brave one. He had died nobly, as a Ramiez should die. And his killer still lived. But not for long.

Don Pablo was elderly. His thick hair was iron-grey. Because he had always been a tall lean man, much taller than Ramon would ever have been, his back was stooped. His face was hawk-like and as brown and wrinkled as old leather. He looked ruthless and imperious and noble and he was all these things. Yes, in his way, even the last of these things. Gringos would call him a robber and a scoundrel but he spat on the opinion of gringos. He had served in the war against the Americans and, although the Americans won and the spoils of Texas were now theirs, to Don Pablo this did not mean a thing. He was still at war with the Americans who treated his people like pigs (only the high-born like himself should be allowed to treat the peons like pigs!). He had his own law and justice.

The Americans had been delivered into his hands. They were the Americans who had brought about the death of his brother. They would pay for this. How terribly they would pay! They would be a long time paying; they would pay in some measure too for all the sins the Americans had committed against the Mexican people.

Don Pablo's Spanish forebears had been experts in torture, their Inquisition had brought torture to a fine art never surpassed before or since. And Don Pablo still had a small collection of their devilish instruments, or replicas of them which had been handed down from father to son. Don Pablo had experimented with these instruments, though in a comparatively small way, from time to time. He had used them as instruments of punishment. He considered torture to be a gentlemanly art . . .

And now he would be able to let himself go, to really attain the greatest of finesse. And perhaps when he had finished with the two Americans he would send their bodies back over the border into their own lands as a warning the way the Apaches used to do.

Ah, those Apaches! He was reminded

of Ben Jagar who had Apache blood in him as well as Mexican and only the Deity knew what else. There was a poet of cruelty and savagery and cunning and vengeance! It was a pity that Ben and his band had left the rancho before the Americans were brought in and that Don Pablo could not reach him now. Ben would have greatly enjoyed the show his old friend meant to put on tonight to assuage his grief and his pain.

Already now, as he crossed to the window of his study he could see his men bringing out the flaming torches and putting them in the sconces around the courtyard walls. The courtyard was only lit up this way on festive occasions, for Don Pablo was always wary of giving enemies too much light to shoot by. This was not really a festive occasion. But it would be more than that: it would be Don Pablo's paean of vengeance, his reassertion of the right of a feudal lord and arbiter of life and death over all who tilled his lands and watched his stock and household or trespassed on his holdings.

The flickering torches bathed the courtyard in a garish shifting light. The men were bringing out the cross, the implements. These were better suited to a cellar, reflected Don Pablo, and a huge masked man stripped to the waist who handled the irons and implements with loving care as he handed them one by one to the inquisitors and the shrieks of the victims echoed and re-echoed. But Don Pablo wanted a show. This would serve as a lesson to some of his more fractious peoples too: the very look of those inquisitorial instruments would be enough to strike fear into superstitious hearts.

Don Pablo realized that, in his relish of expectations, he was forgetting the memory of his brother. He bowed his head once more. He drew the curtains across the window and turned away. With bowed head he went back to his desk. They would tell him when everything was ready.

★　★　★

Jim and Rabby were incarcerated in a vaulted wine cellar lit only by a small hurricane lantern suspended in the ceiling. They were bound hand and foot with thin hemp that cut cruelly into the flesh. They were fastened to stout staples in the wall and separated so that they could not get near to each other. All around them were wine barrels and boxes containing bottles couched in straw. 'The ol' buzzard does himself well,' Rabby Buckthorne had remarked.

The old buzzard had come to see them after they were thrown down here. He had not kicked them or spit on them. He had not even come near to them. He had just stood looking at them, towering over them, looking at them as if they were two animals he had caught. Standing there with his hawk face, beaky nose and crooked back he had seemed like some evil old bird of prey and the shadows fled away from him and palpitated in the corners like terrified little animals. He had told them they would not have too long to wait to face their fate. But that would be only the beginning. He had promised them an exceedingly slow and painful death.

It had, of course, been daylight when the two gringos were thrown into the cellar. There was a small grating high in one wall and through this some light had come. The rest of the light had come from the lantern which had been burning when they were put down there and had been burning ever since.

At first they had looked for ways of escape, for some means to break their bonds. But, at last, they had given this up as hopeless.

They had talked in between periods of silence and the time had passed. Nobody had come near them since Don Pablo left and now there was no dim light from the grating up above and the shadows in the corner were larger and blacker and the gringos knew that night had come.

How much longer? Maybe they would be able to make a break for it when they were taken up. But it seemed a forlorn hope!

6

They looked up when the heavy door opened and neither of them could believe their eyes.

Old Nevada carried his bowie knife like a dagger and, as he moved into the light, the blade glistened with blood. But he wiped it off on his pants before sheering the ropes that bound his friends.

They rose to their feet, massaging themselves, grunting at the agony of returning circulation.

Rabby began: 'Thanks, Nevady, but where in tarnation . . . ?'

'Quiet,' hissed the ancient prospector. 'You ain't outa the woods yet. C'mon.'

They followed him up the steps. He took out his gun and handed it back to Rabby. 'Cover me,' he whispered. 'But don't shoot unless you have to.' He patted the bowie knife. 'Martha's still got a few bites in her.'

In the stone passage above a man lay on his face in a pool of blood. Jim picked up the carbine from by his side. The stock was red and sticky. With a grimace of disgust, Jim wiped it off on his sleeve. But carefully: this was an ancient weapon and quite likely to go off without warning.

They went along the passage and turned a corner and found themselves in a larger room, sparsely-furnished and with a few bunks around the walls as in a barrack room. A man sat on a stool against a wall. He looked up drowzily at Nevada and, by the time he had chance to show surprise, Rabby had him covered. He quivered with fear. Rabby went over to him and hit him on the head with the barrel of the gun and caught him as he fell. Jim helped Rabby to bundle him on to one of the bunks and cover him with a blanket.

'He was asleep when I came by first,' said Nevada. 'That was why I was whispering, so's not to wake him. He might have yelled before we could get to him.'

'Well, he's asleep again now anyway,' said Rabby. Nevada led the way again. Rabby came second, carrying Nevada's gun. Jim brought up the rear. He had a pistol now too, that he had taken from the stunned man. He tucked it in the waistband of his trousers and held on to the carbine. You could do a lot of damage with a carbine if you handled it properly.

'We gotta cross the corner of the courtyard,' said Nevada. 'But luckily it's a part that's in shadow. The rest of it's lit up like a barbecue. We'll keep in single file. Less danger of us being spotted that way.'

'You're the boss,' said Rabby.

'I'm glad to hear you admit it after all these years.'

They went through the door one by one, with a small interval in between. They reached the wall and went along it. The courtyard at their left was ablaze with light but none of it reached this far. A cross was erected up there.

'Don Pablo evidently had something fancy worked out for you two,' said Nevada. 'I allus said the ol' coot was as loco as a drunken Apache.'

They reached the door in the wall. 'This was locked. I bust the lock with my knife.' Nevada opened the door.

There were three horses tethered in a clump of trees outside. 'Now I'm a horse thief too,' said Nevada.

They did not set the beasts to a gallop until they figured they were out of earshot of the house. Then they rode hard until they fetched up at a cave in the hills, an old hideout of Nevada's that he didn't think anyone else knew about.

The two KP men made their thanks again but he brushed these impatiently aside.

'Last time we saw you you were goin' in the opposite direction,' said Rabby.

'Wal, I knew you were chasing Ben Jagar and would probably end up at the rancho. I figured you might need some help. I had nothin' else to do and I hadn't seen any excitement in a coon's age ... Besides, young Rabby, you saved my life once an' I figured I might not have much time left to pay off that debt.'

'Hell, that was when we were only sprigs.'

'You were a sprig you mean. Anyway, I haven't forgotten it. I figured that, 'cos o' you, I bin' livin' on borrowed time for close on sixty years. It's a long time.'

They lit a fire in the cave. Nevada explained that the smoke escaped from various clefts in the roof but not in volume from any particular one. They had to take a chance on it being noticed but he did not think it would be. They took that chance: Jim and Rabby were both badly in need of strong hot coffee. This, spiced with rum that Nevada produced from the back of his patient pack-mule made them feel like new men.

They took it in turns to keep watch

that night. Nevada had cut himself in. The other two had told him the full story of the rustling, the lynching of Curly, their quest for Ben Jagar. Nevada said he had a score to settle with Jagar who had once been responsible for the death of a prospector friend of his. He had never had the urge to be a one-man crusader — but if he could join up with Jim and Rabby . . . It would be like old times to ride with 'young Rabby Buckthorne' again. Jim and Rabby said they would be glad to have him. The two old-timers, scorning sleep at first, and not without some prompting from the curious Jim, talked of days long past. And Jim learned things about his old mentor and friend that he had never heard before.

Rabby and Nevada had been on the owl-hoot together. Nevada was the eldest; Rabby (he was known as Rabby even then) just a kid.

It had all started out with what was little more than a youthful prank. Rabby was a fiddle-footed young cowboy roaming the West, taking jobs whenever and wherever it pleased him. He hit one of these one-horse hilly-billy burgs where a stranger is looked upon with the utmost suspicion. There he had an argument with a smart-alec barman who tried to pass him a bad coin. The barman drew a shotgun. Rabby plugged him in the shoulder. The next step would have been through a lynch-rope: Rabby on the noosed end and most of the mean-looking populace heaving on the other. But Nevada stepped in and shot up the saloon and Rabby and he escaped in the ensuing mêlée.

Nevada didn't know Rabby from Adam but he hated to see a fellow fiddle-footer get a raw deal. Nevada was prospecting even then. He was older than Rabby but, even so, kind of young to be traipsing the lonely trails with a burro and an old horse, grubbing in the earth for meagre sustenance. He had come into this town for supplies and had been keenly aware of its unfriendliness and the sharp methods of its shopkeepers towards any stranger. As he told Rabby, he had been about to shoot the place up anyway.

He meant that too. They were both broke. And Nevada reckoned that town owed 'em something, if only the dollar that the barman bilked Rabby out of. To this they could add wear and tear to their clothing, their persons, their beasts. Nevada's old horse hadn't run so fast since it was a shaver and the burro was back on the trail someplace and if the townsfolk had grabbed it that was another strike against them.

At dead of night they went back. They found the burro and left him in hiding. They raided the saloon and wrecked it and came away with a nice little haul in notes and silver coin. It was the barman who fouled things up again. As they were escaping he took a pot shot at them from an upstairs window. Considering he had one arm in a sling his aim was pretty good. He got

Nevada in the side.

They got away again and holed up in the hills. But by this time Nevada was a dying man. Rabby nursed him and through gentleness (a trait so rare in that lawless land) and patience, finally pulled him through.

When they hit the trail again it was to learn that the zealous townsfolk of that one-horse burg had sworn out a warrant against them and their descriptions were on Wanted posters.

They worked together on remote ranches, dodging the law. Then Nevada got the gold fever again and decided to light out for the deserts and the hills. But Rabby, a cowboy born and bred, couldn't see himself in that kind of life. So the partners parted, friends to the last and went their separate ways.

The law must've forgotten about them. They were just small fry anyway, considering that at that time the West was over-run with road agents, rustlers, killers.

Granted that he had saved Nevada's

life in the cabin in the hill those countless years ago, said Rabby, as the two old men sat in the cave with Jim Raine. But hadn't Nevada already, before that, saved Rabby's neck from a lynch-rope? And now Nevada, after all these years, had saved Rabby's neck again, not to mention that of Jim Raine too. According to this, Nevada was still one up on Rabby. Stuff an' nonsense, said Nevada. Anyway, Rabby and Jim would more than repay him for anything he had done by letting him ride along with them and take what came. Since he got old he had begun to get tired of riding the lonely trails.

Jim said as far as he was concerned Nevada could be with them until he plumb faded away the way old prospectors were supposed to do: the KP too would be glad to have him, if only to keep that other mossy-horn, Rabby, out of their hair.

★ ★ ★

Pinto Gap was dead on the border, straddling it. It had little or no law. The marshal was a drunken tramp whom the powers-that-be had long since forgotten. He lived on hand-outs and rot-gut and people could do as they pleased in his town.

Pinto Gap was 'wide-open'. A haven for all the outlaws and cut-throats of this most lawless border region. If the American law chased a man to here — a thing that rarely happened anyway — he could light out in the other direction and be in Mexico and safe from their hands.

Rabby and Jim didn't know this town at all but Nevada did. He said that Ben Jagar and his boys often hung out here. So the three partners had to go wary. They entered the place at night.

There was no street lighting to speak of but the honky-tonks and like establishments made up for this deficiency by blazing like Xmas trees. Except for the red-light houses none of them had drawn blinds and the yellow glare streamed out into the baked cart-rutted street and by contrast the shadowy parts were darker, menacing.

The three partners kept to the shadowy parts while, walking beside their horses, they looked the place over. Nevada had got a horse from some-place. He had left his two burros back in the hills and aimed to look for a likely customer to take them off his hands. All his tackle went with them too, if anybody wanted to set them-selves up as a prospector. Nevada said he was finished with gold-grubbing. All he had ever found was small pockets of dust, barely enough to keep him in vittles. If he hit a big strike now he wouldn't know what to do with it.

The three partners 'did' the town pretty quickly. There wasn't anything much of it. They didn't see anybody they recognized, except one drunken old coot who hailed Nevada. They finished up finally at the livery stables kept by a fat Mex with a wall eye.

They parked their horses for a feed

and a rubdown. Before they left the dark, stinking place, Nevada asked the man if he was in the market for a couple of burros. The Mex said 'if the *señor* would let him see the burros . . . ' Nevada said all right, he'd bring them round in daylight sometime.

The three partners went to a hashhouse for a meal and, after that, on to a saloon. This was the biggest establishment in a town bristling with places of entertainment, whether you wanted gambling, dancing, girls, singing, or just plain drinking. This place had all of these things and it was called The Don Amigo. Despite the Mex-sounding name the clientele seemed to be mainly American, whereas many of the smaller places dealt mainly with Mexicans who eyed with disfavour any gringo who poked his nose inside. There were a few of the better-dressed type of Mexican in The Don Amigo, this kind were pretty powerful along the border, but no scruffy-looking peons.

A small band consisting of piano,

squeeze-box, banjo and kettle-drum was playing music for a scantily-clad female who sang and pranced on the stage to the left of the long bar. There were plenty of tables and chairs and a square of dance-floor. Nobody was dancing at the moment. Most of the males present were watching the singer. But the dance-floor was full of people, both male and female. Not able to get a seat at a table or a place at the bar, they stood drinks in hand and talked and jostled and laughed and shamelessly kissed and cuddled beneath the harsh lights, the blue tobacco mist, the swirling fan which fought a losing battle with the atmosphere. The large room was redolent with the smell of spilled liquor, of cheap scent, of tobacco smoke and dust and sweating human flesh.

Jim, Rabby and Nevada elbowed their way to the bar, looking about them all the time. Old Nevada brought up the rear. His sharp eyes, trained by many years of staring into wide-open spaces, did not miss much. A few people hailed him, elderly people like himself, prospectors and suchlike.

The three men reached the bar and Jim called for the drinks. A sweating half-breed barman, one of three, served them. They took their liquor over into a corner and, their backs to the wall, surveyed the milling faces.

Three thirsty men finished their first drinks quickly and Rabby pushed his way back to the bar. This time he said he would bring the bottle. He was as good as his word. But when he returned his wizened monkey-face no longer wore a smile.

'Just seen somebody I useter know,' he said.

'Who?' said Nevada.

'Useter call himself Ponch Bates. Useter ride with Ben Jagar.'

'He still calls himself Ponch Bates,' said Nevada. 'And as far as I know, he still rides with Ben Jagar. Did he see you?'

'I don't think so. He's over at the

corner of the bar. You can see him if you lean this way a bit.'

Jim too joined Nevada in his new position and then all three men could get a glimpse of the subject of the conversation. He was middle-aged and running to fat. His sombrero was held by a thong in the Mexican way and at the moment hung at his shoulders. His head was completely hairless, lending a last obscene touch to his ugly face.

'It's Ponch all right,' said Nevada.

'I've never seen him before,' said Jim.

Rabby said: 'That sidewinder was making a name for himself as a killer before you were born, younker.' Nevada said: 'Folks used to say that when Ponch was about Ben Jagar was never very far away. They left this territory together. Looks like they came back together.'

Rabby said: 'I wonder if he knows I'm connected with the KP Ranch now?'

'You ran him off didn't you? You . . . '

'He's moving,' cut in Jim.

'Watch him!'

They watched him. They followed him, Rabby thoughfully corking the bottle and putting it in his own pocket.

For all his squat bulk, he moved pretty fast. And he had a clearer passage to the door than the partners had. Had he spotted them, they wondered.

When they got out into the night, he was nowhere to be seen.

7

'Spread out,' said Rabby. 'We make too big a target this way.'

'Get out of the light,' said Jim.

They moved apart, seeking out the shadows. And not a second too soon. The night was suddenly hideous with gunfire. Nevada cursed hoarsely as a slug burned his arm. Rabby, throwing himself for the meagre cover of a hitching rail, misjudged, hit his head on the post. He blacked out momentarily. Coming to his senses he saw that Jim was beside him.

'You all right, Rabby?'

'Sure.' Rabby nodded his head vigorously, dispelling the fog too. Any other words he might have spoken would have been drowned as Jim opened up now, sending a stream of lead to the shadows across the road. Out of the corner of his eye Rabby saw

Nevada crouching a short distance away. The old prospector was apparently unhurt.

Flame stabbed the darkness. Rabby hugged the boardwalk as bullets came perilously close. He figured there were at least three snipers over there. They had the element of surprise too. If the three partners had not separated when they had they might be dead mutton by now. If Ponch Bates was back of this bushwhack parlay he had certainly got some reinforcements purty-damn-quick.

Jim had lost his hat. His lips were drawn back whitely from his teeth in the half-light. Rabby yelled at him:

'We gotta move from here!'

They ran for the deeper shadows. They crouched low, running away from the bushwhackers, drawing the fire off Nevada. Rabby, bringing up the rear, cursed as a lump of leather was shot from his boot. He sprawled. Jim grabbed him, dragged him around the corner.

Nevada was following them but he had further to come. Jim and Rabby covered him from their corner. Rabby had to stop to reload. Jim stepped out, grabbed Nevada by an arm and literally slung him into the covering darkness.

Nevada demanded to know whose side 'this young hellion' was on — almost broke his gosh-durned neck! He had a small bullet-burn on his left elbow but otherwise he was all right.

There was a lull in the firing. 'Quit yapping, you ol' goat,' said Jim. 'Have you got plenty slugs?'

'Sure, wisht I had a rifle though.'

The three men loaded their guns. 'How about tryin' to flank 'em?' said Jim.

Both oldsters were agreeable. They didn't like being pinned down like flies.

'One at a time,' said Jim. 'I'll go first.' He went.

They were out of the aura of lights now. Jim scuttled half-crouching across the dark street. The bushwhackers opened up at him. Rabby and Nevada retaliated, covering him. Jim hit the opposite sidewalk, rolling. He seemed to have come through a hail of lead; his ears drummed. He crouched against a dark log wall, surprised to find himself all in one piece. He fanned the hammer of his gun, sending a stream of lead along the boardwalk. Out of the corner of his eye, he saw one of his partners running, he couldn't be sure which one. The man faltered. Jim stepped out. A slug whipped at his shirt-front; perilously near. The man came on again, limping. Rabby!

'Twisted my damned ankle,' he grumbled. Jim cursed him roundly, affectionately, with relief.

It sounded as if the bushwhackers were drawing off. Nevada scuttled across the street and only a couple of random shots were thrown at him and he arrived unhurt.

People were beginning to show themselves tentatively at lighted windows and doors. The three partners began to advance along the board-walk, spread out cautiously. Bootheels hammered ahead of them. Rabby said:

'They aimed to get us all in one bundle but they were a mite too hasty an' it didn't work. Now they don't want to show their faces.'

Jim was well ahead now of the two elderly men. Even if he heard what Rabby said he gave no sign of doing so. He moved like a mountain cat after a kill.

Hoofbeats hammered, faded quickly into the night. Jim stopped. His two companions caught up with him.

'And we didn't get a single one of 'em,' said Jim disgustedly.

'Shooting in the dark ain't good,' said Nevada. 'Even for a professional gunslinger like yourself.'

'I ain't no professional gunslinger,' said Jim.

'Well, you certainly handle yourself like one.' There was no mockery in Nevada's voice, only a note of praise.

The three partners were pretty sure now that the bushwhackers had been

Ben Jagar's men, egged on by Ponch Bates. Ben himself would not be among them. He left that kind of job to hirelings.

People were moving out into the street. Rabby said:

'We better make ourselves scarce, too. We don't want to draw any awkward questions, or even more bullets.'

They withdrew across the street and around the dark corner that had given them shelter before. They moved along the 'backs' of Pinto Gap. Nobody followed them. The people of the town had discovered that there were no dead bodies lying in the street and they had gone back to their boozing, their gambling, their love-making. They were too cautious of their own skins to be getting too nosey. The marshal, a lawman by title only, lay on the bunk in back of his office in a drunken stupor. It was doubtful whether he had even heard the shooting. And it was certain sure that nobody would bother him about it.

Jim, Rabby and Nevada found a lodging-house on the edge of town and entered. An over-ripe redheaded female led them upstairs. The place was not overclean but they had seen worse beds. They refused the woman's offer of a drink (or anything else they needed!). All they wanted to do was sleep.

They had a biggish room. Rabby and Nevada shared a huge sagging four-poster which had probably been bought cheap from some impoverished hacienda. Jim had the little truckle bed up the corner. He was near the window and the moonlight — when the moon decided to come out from behind the lowering clouds — slanted on to the foot of his bed.

* * *

It must have been the sound of the opening window that disturbed him. But, by the time he was fully awake, the man had his head and shoulders inside and the gun in his fist was pointing at the four-poster bed in which the two oldsters snored. Jim had his gun close to his hand. The man turned his body, his gun. Maybe he had been told where the third cowboy was. Or maybe he had only just noticed Jim. Either way he was a mite too late. Jim pumped two slugs into him and he toppled headfirst into the room. When he came to rest, lay still, only the bottom halves of his legs were out of the window.

Rabby, who was nearest, hit the floor with a crash as Nevada pushed him. The hoary prospector shot over his old pard's back and came to rest on his backside.

'It's all right, you two ol' goats,' said Jim: His words were humorous but the tone of his voice wasn't.

Rabby and Nevada sorted themselves out, rose. By this time Jim was at the window, cautiously leaning out. He could not see anything. The sniper had reached the window by climbing up the convenient roof of a lean-to.

From the centre of town sound drifted. Some of the joints were still open. Lights went on here and there nearer to Jim. The more law-abiding towns-folk, shopkeepers and the like who lived this end of town, didn't like being awakened in the middle of the night even in Pinto Gap.

Out there somebody yelled, 'What's going on?'

Jim yelled back, 'It's all right. I just shot a rat. The biggest man-eating brute you ever saw.'

Some of the lights went out again. These people's capacity for minding their own business was truly remarkable. Rabby lit the lamp in the biggish room. Jim closed the window and joined his two partners over the body of the man he had shot. One slug had got him in the chest, the other in the throat. He was not a pretty sight and already the floor around him was swimming with blood from the torn jugular.

He was a palpable half-breed, and a pretty dirty-looking specimen at that.

Rabby and Jim said they had not seen him before. Nevada grimaced, said: 'The face looks familiar. I've probably seen him with Ben Jagar at some time or other.'

Jim said: 'It don't need no detective to figure out that this is one of Jagar's men.'

'And Ben does rather favour half-breeds in his band,' said Rabby. ' 'Cos he's a breed himself I suppose, an outcast who gathers other outcasts to him . . . On the other hand, some of Pablo Ramiez's boys could have got here by now. He might be one of them. He might even be in Pinto Gap on his lonesome. You killed a man back at the rancho, Nevada. This could be his brother or his cousin or somep'n — you know how these people are.'

'Hell,' spluttered Nevada. 'Why do yuh hafta go an' complicate things? Ain't we got enough trouble with Jagar's boys without dragging Ramiez into it again?'

Jim had put his pants on. He moved

nearer to the door. Then, with a violent movement he flung it open. He grabbed at something in the darkness there. He disappeared from view for a moment. When he reappeared again there was somebody else with him. A female figure, but definitely not the redheaded battle-axe they had seen earlier that night.

Jim had her by the arm and although she struggled she could not escape. She was slim and young and of dark exotic beauty. She wore only a thin dressing gown of some soft blue stuff over a white nightdress. The gown flew wide open. But Jim did not seem to have noticed any of this or the way the girl's fine dark eyes blazed at him. His own blazed and he said furiously:

'What were you doing out there?'

'What did you expect? All this shooting. Let me go. I . . . '

She broke off with a little cry as she caught sight of the bloody corpse on the floor. She put her clenched fist into her mouth and bit into the knuckles.

Her teeth were small and white, her lips full, red, well-shaped. All of her was well-shaped.

She turned her head away but she stopped struggling and Jim let her go. The young man had begun to get a little sheepish now he had had a good look at what he had caught. He had acted hastily, caught up in the savagery of the last few moments in this violent night. The girl was obviously unarmed, a weak female, and, like most right-thinking Westerners Jim had an inherent chivalry.

The girl did not bolt now, though she kept her head averted from the gory sight on the floor. Though the hot-eyed young man had scared her, she seemed to have been reassured by the sight of the two elderly persons in long underwear who stood blinking owlishly at her. She did not seem put out by the sight of their state of half-dress or, indeed, her own similar state. She looked far more charming than the three men did. No man caught in long underwear in the small hours is at his handsomest or his best.

She stood there, seemed to be waiting for some explanation.

But now more noises came through the half-open door. Jim, acting instinctively again, though perhaps not quite so violently as before, went back to it.

There were about half-a-dozen people in the passage now. They backed away fearfully when they saw his gun. The redheaded woman was not among them, which fact Jim thought rather strange. An old man with a bristle of white hair like a turkey-cock's comb pushed himself forward now. He ignored the gun.

'Where's my daughter?' he bristled.

'I'm in here, Dad,' called the girl from behind Jim. The oldster, faded dressing gown, busted slippers and all brushed past the young man at the door and entered the room. Jim could not help but admire the old turkey's guts. He let him go and snarled at the rest:

'Any of yuh know where the red-headed woman is who looks after this place?'

They looked at each other. A scared-looking youth said, 'I saw you an' the other two men with her. Then, afterwards, I saw her go out. I haven't seen her since.'

Nobody else was helpful. 'I suggest you folks go back to bed,' said Jim.

Nobody argued. They drifted away. Jim went back into the room and, for the time being, closed the door behind him. Rabby was telling the turkey-oldster what had happened. The latter seemed somewhat mollified. His daughter stood beside him and held his hand. Her face was cameo-like and beautiful.

'I know that scum,' said the turkey gent, indicating the man on the floor. 'Another no-good like so many people in this town.'

'D'yuh know Ben Jagar?' Rabby asked.

'More scum! I know him. But not to speak to.'

'Ever seen this man with Ben?'

'All the scum in this town hangs around Ben Jagar when he's here.'

'D'yuh know if Ben's in town now?'

'Couldn't say.'

Jim cut in now. 'Where's the big redheaded woman hang out?'

The turkey gent turned. 'Well, now, that's funny. I'm surprised she ain't here now. She sleeps on this floor. Her room's just down the hall . . . And she don't like people shooting her place up as a rule.'

'This is her place then?'

'I've always figured it was. Her husband ran it before he died. She's run it herself ever since. Two-three years. Her husband was a Mexican,' mused the old man. 'I'm certainly surprised Sal ain't here by now. Everybody else was.'

'This husband of hers,' said Jim. 'He didn't die from lead-poisoning by any chance?'

'That's kind of a funny question to ask. But I know what you mean. No, he died peaceably in his bed. Pneumonia. As far as I know he was a peaceable man or, at least, as peaceable as any man can afford to be in this town.'

'Which room did you say this Sal sleeps in?'

The oldster hesitated for a moment. Then he said, 'Next but two.'

'Thanks,' said Jim. He left the room, closing the door behind him. Nobody followed him.

The hall was silent now, though there were sounds of movement behind the closed doors as he passed them. Reflecting now, Jim decided that the girl back there had as much guts as her Pa. The way she had come along to investigate the shooting, and got there first too! Unless . . .

But now he was at the door he sought. It was closed. He pressed his ear to it. There was no sound. He tried the door and found it locked.

Before knocking with his left hand, he took out his gun. There might be somebody in there with the woman, lying doggo, waiting.

There was no answer to his knock. 'Open up,' he called recklessly. There was no reply. He put his shoulder to the door and heaved. It creaked agonisingly. He increased the pressure. He was a lusty young specimen.

Behind the closed doors all around him there were murmurings and shiftings. But here there was nothing. Jim was irritated. He backed to the other side of the passage. Then he flung himself against the silent door.

It caved, burst open. He staggered into darkness. He flung himself sideways, down. Nothing happened. He crouched on the floor, feeling rather foolish.

He rose, stood for a moment to get his eyes accustomed to the darkness. It was much deeper here because the curtains were drawn. The shine of glass on a lamp caught his eye. He had no matches; he groped, found a box on the table near the lamp. He lit the lamp.

His gun was ready as the light

blossomed about him. The room was empty. It looked feminine, smelled feminine. The bed was empty. It did not look as if it had been slept in. The door had been locked on the outside then! Where had the big redhead gone?

The room told Jim nothing. He began to feel a little sheepish again, though he wouldn't have admitted it for worlds. He retraced his steps slowly. The door of his own room was still closed. He was almost there when he heard footsteps on the stairs behind him.

He turned on stocking feet. He was sheepish no longer, more like a prowling wolf, lean, young, very dangerous. Gun in hand, he went back along the passage to the head of the stairs.

8

He came face to face with the big redheaded woman. She saw the gun in his hand and stopped.

'What's the idea?' she demanded hoarsely.

Jim did not say anything at first, hc just looked at her. They stood staring at each other wordlessly. She was dressed in her finery, all the frills and furbelows of the day. She looked different to when Jim had seen her earlier that evening. Though rather overblown, running to seed, she was still a handsome woman.

'What is this,' she said, her voice harsh now, 'some kind of hold-up?' She did not seem scared. Or surprised to see Jim there like this. Either there were no grounds for his suspicions or she was a good actress. Jim became a little uncertain. He seemed to be fated to continue making a fool of himself this night. He lowered the gun. He went the whole hog; demanded:

'Where've *you* been?'

'I can't see as that's any of your business.'

'A man's been killed here while you've been out.'

Her eyes widened then. She said almost involuntarily it seemed, 'I've been to visit a sick friend.'

'Kind of funny time to come home isn't it?' said Jim. He almost asked whether the 'sick friend' was male or female but his inherent courtesy forbade him from going too far and the words were never uttered.

But the woman might have been reading his mind. 'What do you mean by that?' she shrilled.

She came on up the stairs, ignoring the gun. Jim thought at first she meant to lay violent hands on him. He did not know what he would have done. But she stopped again, glaring up at him. He saw now that her eyes were green, and a little bleary.

He had not answered her. And now she said: 'If you must know, my friend drifted off to sleep and I figured I ought to get back here and get some shut-eye myself. There's plenty of work here in the mornings. Early too. A place like this doesn't run itself. What are you, some kind of detective or something? Who's this who has been killed?'

'You better take a look.' Jim turned. She followed him along the passage without another word. Everybody turned as they entered the bedroom. The big woman, Sal, seemed surprised to see so many people there. She said:

'Howdy, Mr Calhoun. Howdy, Ella.'

The old man with the turkey-comb front-piece answered her. So did his daughter. They both called her 'Sal'.

She saw the body on the floor and said 'My Gosh' but that was all. She was pretty hard-bitten.

'Know him?' asked Jim.

'Face looks familiar. One of the town hardcases I guess.' She looked towards old Calhoun again and it was he who told her what had happened, or, at least, what Rabby had told him about this.

She heard him out. Then her hard-bitten gaze swept over the other men. She said:

'And it seemed he meant to kill you?'

It was Rabby who answered; quickly, before reckless Jim could open his mouth. 'He could have just been after pickings o' course. But he had a gun in his hand when he got through the window so naturally Jim plugged him before he could do any harm with it.'

She turned and looked at the young hellion behind her. 'Yeh, I plugged him,' he said. 'What would you have done? He had only had to open up and my two partners would have woken up dead.'

She smiled faintly. 'I'd've done the same I guess. I keep a gun in my bedroom too.' Was that some kind of warning? She became suddenly brisk. 'He's no loss to the community I guess. First thing we gotta do is get him out of here — he's making a mess on the floor.'

'We'll take care of it,' said Rabby.

'There's a broken-down shed in the yard. It isn't used for anything now. Put him in there.' She turned towards the dark girl. 'You look all in, Ella. You ought to get back to bed.'

'She's going right now,' said old Calhoun. 'Come on, honey.'

The girl said 'Goodnight' quickly, hardly looking at the men. It was as if she had become suddenly conscious of her state of half-undress. Jim felt he ought to apologise to her. But he let the opportunity pass and her father ushered her from the room.

Sal said briskly, 'Looks like I got back just at the right time.'

Jim said: 'She's been visiting a sick friend.' He wondered if the words sounded as foolish to his friends as they did to him. Neither of them said anything.

'Old lady down with a bad attack of the croup,' said Sal. 'No kith or kin in this hell-hole.'

She did not look like a good Samaritan or a Lady Bountiful. But Jim wondered if she was telling the truth after all. Probably there were ways of finding out.

Rabby said: 'We'll see to everything, ma'am. If you've been sitting up half the night I daresay you're tired.'

'I am.' She seemed to reflect for a moment. Then she said, 'This'll have to be reported to the law first thing in the morning. Just to keep things straight from my point of view.'

'We've no objection to that, ma'am.'

'Couldn't get that drunken old coot, Cromer, out of bed now without using a charge of dynamite anyway,' she said. She seemed to come to a decision. 'I'll leave it to you, gentlemen.' She turned briskly and marched from the room.

Jim closed the door after her. 'She's a cool customer.'

'Yeh,' said Nevada. This was the first word he had spoken for some time.

'Know much about her?'

'Nothing at all.'

'Come on,' said Rabby. He pulled a face. 'Let's get this chore finished with.'

They wrapped the body in an old blanket they found, saying they would pay for it, such as it was, if Sal objected. They carried their gruesome burden down the stairs and out through the back door into the yard. Rabby and Jim did the carrying. Nevada brought up the rear, a gun in his hand. Other would-be snipers might be lurking around.

But nothing happened and they parked the body in the shed and left it there. They found a pail and a mop in the bathroom and they cleaned up the mess in their room. Finally they were finished, though the smell of carbolic was still not strong enough to kill the smell of blood and death. Neither of them slept again that night. They lay awake smoking and talking desultorily. They chewed over theories that led them exactly noplace. They finished up with the same resolve as before; they must get Ben Jagar! And the sooner the better; before he got them! Could be Pablo Ramiez was still in the running too!

*　*　*

They were up early but, even so, the proprietress had beaten them to it. She was dressed for work, blowsy, her hair a flaming mop.

'You ain't seen the marshal have you, ma'am?' asked Rabby.

'Nope,' she said. 'Heck, I'm too busy. Cromer's probably still dead to the world anyway. Besides, I figured you boys 'ud go down and see him as soon as you've had breakfast.'

'Yeh, we'll do that, ma'am.'

She was more affable than they had expected her to be. They would not have been surprised had she given them notice to get out of the place. She seemed to have accepted the story they told her last night. Even Jim began to think he had misjudged her.

Sick friend! Aw, hell — why not?

The food was good and hot. Bacon, beans, eggs, fried bread; frijoles, done beautifully, with hot maple syrup; lashings of hot strong coffee. They complimented the lady. 'All my own work,' she said cheerfully. Sal might be sloppy and blowsy but she could certainly cook.

They had a smoke. They did not bother to visit the stiff victim of last night's little fracas but went right down to the marshal's office.

This was a sagging clapboard with a log jail in back. The cell-block looked even more disused than the front part: a child could have busted out of it. Law in Pinto Gap was a blatant mockery.

They tried the office door and found it locked. Rabby knocked upon it. There was no answer, no sound from inside. Pinto Gap was only just sluggishly coming alive. A few bleary-eyed people looked curiously at the three men but nobody stopped or spoke. Rabby knocked again, louder.

He might have been thumping on the door of a tomb for all the satisfaction he got.

Jim took out his gun. First of all he emptied it of bullets. It was on a hair-trigger and he didn't want it to go off in his hand. Then he reversed the weapon and hammered on the door with the walnut and metal butt. The noise was enough to awaken even the occupants of a tomb. It did the trick too. A voice shouted something unintelligible inside.

Jim quit his racket. Feet shuffled the other side of the door. There was the sound of bolts being shot. The door was flung open.

A pot-bellied middle-aged man stood there. He was in shirt and trousers, the shirt open wide down the front, revealing a hairy, flabby chest. His face was red and bloated, his eyes bleary. He had a chewed fragment of grey moustache which might once have been a real old Western walrus like all the best lawmen wear. His sparse hair was like dirty tangled straw. He was an unprepossessing sight.

A big Frontier-model Colt shook in his meaty hand.

'We come in peace, you can put away the gun.' There was an edge in Jim Raine's voice. He had holstered his own weapon.

'Marshal Cromer?' enquired Rabby in a more conciliatory tone of voice.

The man peered at them owlishly, suspiciously. Then slowly he lowered his gun and finally tucked it into the waistband of his trousers. The trousers were so tight across his sagging stomach that his task was not easy. His movements were uncertain and lacked co-ordination. Jim Raine reflected sardonically that if the gun went off now the fat man would blow his own toes off. But the man finally made it and looked up owlishly again and said:

'Yeh, I'm Marshal Cromer. What d'yuh want?'

Rabby got in his two-cents worth first. 'We want to report an attempted robbery and a killing. If we could come into the office for a moment, marshal, we'll make a formal statement.'

Cromer hadn't had a 'formal statement' made to him in years. He backed before Rabby like a fat automaton and next moment the three visitors were in the office, the door shut behind them.

The place was a dusty shambles. Cromer swept papers from his desk on to the floor. They were reward dodgers that he had not bothered to tack up as he should have done. Doubtless he had not even looked at them — no doubt some of the faces of those tin-types, those descriptions could be seen quite frequently in town.

Rabby did most of the talking. He should have been a senator or salesman or something. The armed burglar, the law-abiding shooting in self-defence; too bad the man was dead, but people who broke into private premises had to risk that didn't they? Rabby wrote out the statement on a piece of grimy paper the marshal found for him. The old owlhooter and wrangler had had no schooling but he taught himself to write as a young man and, over the years, his copper-plate script had improved. There was yet none of the squiggly infirmities of age; and Rabby spelled good too. Both Nevada and Marshal Cromer were blinded by the science of this *tour de force*.

The marshal didn't ask many questions. He didn't have much chance. They chivvied him from outside the half-open door of his living-quarters. They got him outside and they chivvied him down to the lodging house to view the body. He was grumbling all the while that he hadn't had his breakfast yet. People looked after them. Curious, apprehensive; some of them grinning. Looked like the marshal was being made to earn his keep at last: a good sign for some, a bad one for others.

Sal was ready with hot coffee. She was still affable, she even joshed the grumbling marshal along a bit. But she kept giving Jim sidelong and meaningful glances. Jim could not make out whether these were meant to be threatening or coquettish — although the woman was almost old enough to be his mother. He remembered that she had given him the same kind of looks over breakfast and Rabby, intercepting some of them, had grinned wickedly. Jim had thought he was in for some leg-pulling but, when they got outside, Rabby seemed to have forgotten the matter.

Suddenly the young man got a vague idea of what might be the meaning of Sal's profound glances. He had busted her door open last night. This had not done the lock much good. Sal must have guessed he was the culprit. He had forgotten about the incident again until just now. Did she mean to sic the marshal on to him? What would he do if she did? What would the marshal do? Jim couldn't shoot the drunken fat coot.

But Sal did not say anything. She did not follow the men out to the tumbledown shed.

Last night the three men had propped the sagging door shut with a piece of loose timber. It was just as they had left it. The shed was not an ideal undertaking parlour. Jim shifted the timber and the door swung open of its own accord. Jim stepped aside to let the others file in first, the marshal now leading the way. Sal's hot coffee had revived him a bit and he was trying to act official. Strutting, carrying his paunch before him like a swollen badge of office.

There was not room for all of them — and the marshal's belly to boot — in the interior of the shed. The corpse took up quite a bit of room too, as they remembered, and might already have begun to stink. So Jim and Nevada stayed outside while Rabby and Cromer entered the dim, dusty place.

They heard the so-called lawman make an explosive exclamation. Then Rabby came out again, the fat man at his heels. Rabby looked stupefied.

'*The body ain't there!*'

'Horsefeathers,' said Jim and went into the shed himself.

He was in there longer than the other two. When he came out he was shaking his head and scowling.

'The blanket we wrapped him in has gone too. All that's left is a dried-up pool of blood.'

The marshal entered the shed again and was shown the blood by Jim. The lawman was then convinced that there had been a bleeding carcase there fairly recently. Besides, Sal claimed to have seen the body last night too, and the marshal could check up with old Calhoun and his daughter if he wanted to.

'Are you sure he was dead?'

'Hell! Of course he was dead. He had two slugs in him. One in the chest and one in the throat. He didn't have enough blood left in him to keep a snail alive.'

'That's right sure 'nough.'

'Mebbe somebody dragged him out

back a bit,' said the marshal.

When he was sober he had a whining cantankerous streak. And right now he needed a drink real bad.

9

They beat the weeds back of the house. The morning wind brought a sweet scent from off the plains. There was no savour of blood and death now. They did not find the missing body.

They retraced their steps to the broken-down shed, the tomb that had given up its dead to wander abroad.

But not without help: that was certain sure!

They examined the ground in front of the shed and they found hoof-marks. In a patch of softer soil further away the marks were deeper. Judging by their shape this was when the horse had been going away from the shed. Seemed like he had been quite heavily laden too.

So that was that; Johnny Bushwhacker's friend — or friends — had called for him pronto. They had worked quietly and, as the shed was some distance from the house they had gone unheard and undetected.

The four men went back into the house to carry the news to Sal, who evinced as much surprise as everybody else had. Old Calhoun and his daughter were there now. They corroborated the story too that there had indeed been a body, and a very dead one.

Despite her disturbed night, Ella Calhoun, in a shirtwaist and skirt, looked just as beautiful as when the partners saw her last. Her glossy black hair was around her shoulders. Her eyes were bright.

She treated Jim the same way she treated the other three men, with courtesy and friendliness. If she remembered his pugnacious behaviour of the night before, she did not seem to hold it against him.

Sal had fixed breakfast for the marshal, which fact made him a much brighter man. He got it down with a will. Then, with thanks, excused himself. No doubt, after all that, he needed a drink. He told the partners that he would 'make enquiries'. They doubted whether these enquiries, even if they were made, would come to anything. But they did not say so. Even Jim Raine bade Marshal Cromer quite an affable 'So-long'. He would not be of any help to them in their quest; but at least he would not get in their way.

None of the people who had seen the dead bushwhacker had known who he was, although he had looked familiar to them. The marshal had not been able to tell anything from the description they had given him, or, if he had, had not said so. There were so many half-breeds who could answer to that description slouching around the town.

Old Calhoun, it appeared, kept a general store and his daughter helped him, looking after the women customers. Old Calhoun, it seemed, had been an Indian fighter. But he was old now and a man had to settle down some time. He still hated Indians. But not Mexicans, although he knew many

Americans still hated Mexicans. He had had a Mexican wife. She had been dead these ten years. A high-born lady, his daughter took after her. His daughter did not happen to be in the room when he said this. He said this himself — but the boys got much more information after his daughter and he had left the house. This included the fact that Calhoun's late wife had been a member of the Ramiez clan, a close relation of Pablo Ramiez in fact.

This was an interesting and rather startling fact and the boys didn't quite know what to make of it. Did Calhoun and his beautiful half-Mexican daughter still keep in touch with the Ramiez clan? And would they help Pablo Ramiez or his friends if need be?

If Johnny Bushwhacker's friends had, ostensibly, taken his body away so he would not be identified and connected with them, had they had any inside help? Had old Calhoun been lying when he said he did not know the man, had not known him? These questions were bound to flash through the pardners' minds, though they did not voice them in front of Sal. Maybe she had the same kind of suspicions and that was why she had given the three men some kind of lead. But she did not voice any suspicions herself either.

Calhoun and his daughter had seemed such a grand couple. Had they strong family loyalties, the kind of loyalties that were in the main much stronger in Mexicans than in Americans?

The three partners met the others of Sal's lodgers, though Jim had caught at least a glimpse of most of them last night. They eyed him in particular very warily; they were an uninteresting and harmless bunch.

They were people who made their living off Pinto Gap through working in stores, offices and suchlike and were tolerated by the rougher element, that virtually ruled the town, because of this. They knew they had to sing small and, above all, never ask questions.

They had brought their hear-nothing, see-nothing, say-nothing facilities to a fine art and they gave Jim, Rabby and Nevada no trouble at all.

The three partners left the lodging-house and went for a meander around the town. They took in every sector of it. By daylight it was even less prepossessing than it had been the night before. They did not see anybody they knew or recognized.

They got themselves some dry chow and filled their water-bottles. They rode their horses from the livery stable and out into the plains. It was a hot cloudless day and far ahead of them half-hidden by a blue haze they could see the craggy range of hills called the Crackerjacks. Rabby and Jim had passed through these after leaving the KP Ranch on the first lap of their quest for vengeance. They were, however, very far away from that point now, for the Crackerjacks sprawled like a spikey-backed, sleeping lizard for many miles along that lawless borderland.

This was the owlhooters paradise. Plenty of wild cover in the Crackerjacks. And, on the American side of the border small towns and ranches to be pillaged. And, on this side the wide-open town of Pinto Gap and, beyond that, the border itself. No wonder Ben Jagar, though once driven away, had returned to this happy hunting ground . . . and elected sardonically to let his old enemies know of his return in the worst way he could think of. Jim Raine's young brother, Curly, had gone like a lamb to his slaughter . . . a plugged peso, Ben's old sign, tossed carelessly beside the violated body.

The three men — two of them with an indomitable purpose, the other tagging along just for the hell of it — rode on towards the Crackerjacks. If Ben and his boys were not in Pinto Gap there was a good possibility that they were somewhere in the Crackerjacks or that, there in the hills, the partners might get a lead on them. They might be riding right to their own death, to die as Curly had died. But they had to take that chance. Back in town Ben could keep tags on them and, when night fell, try another bushwhack parley which this time might prove successful.

They might, for all they knew, have Ramiez's men to contend with too, and Creation knew who or what else. Out here in the open spaces nobody could keep tabs on them and, even if they did run into something up in the hills they could give a good account of themselves. They were outdoor men, all three of them! The town had made them feel cramped and ill-at-ease, wondering what lay around each corner, feeling that every man's hand was against them in that hell-hole of intrigue and lawlessness.

* * *

When they reached the rocks the sun was a vibrating copper gong high in a yellow sky. The heat rebounded from the rocks; its rays were penetrating; they pulled their hats well over their eyes to protect themselves from its glare.

They bivouaced in the shade of a huge boulder and dined frugally on dry biscuits and bully beef washed down with cool water. They smoked. The horses had found a small patch of grass and were regaling themselves too. It was all very peaceful. But for how long? Men had been killed. How many more would be killed before the quest was over, and would these three men, smoking so quietly now in perfect companionship be among the unsung dead?

They arose after a while and continued on their way, the horses picking their way gingerly now over an uneven surface as they slowly climbed all the time. They found signs here and there of other people having passed this way, men and beasts. Then, looking back, Rabby said quietly:

'We're being followed.'

Nevada and Jim looked back too, looked downwards. On the plain below them was a solitary man on a horse.

'Maybe he ain't following us,' said Nevada. 'He's taking an awful chance — one man dogging three. He might've known we'd spot him as soon as we got up here.'

'Mebbe you're right,' agreed Rabby. 'I wonder who it is?'

His two companions could not help him on that. The three of them continued to forge ahead. When they looked back a little later the stranger was still there, although he did not seem to be pushing much and had not appreciably gained on them. From the distance he looked like any other saddle-tramp with no particular place to go and all the time in the world to get there. Probably that was just what he was. He could be an American, a Mexican, or even an Indian. He could be anything or anybody. They tried to dismiss him from their thoughts but every now and then one or the other of them glanced surreptitiously over his shoulder. Until Rabby, who despite his age had remarkably sharp eyes, said:

'He's gone.'

Then they all looked round again and Nevada said, 'He'll be starting to climb now. I guess we'll spot him again a bit later on.'

The horses were finding it hard going. Finally the three men halted the beasts and sat in their saddles and debated what to do. Normally they would have tethered the horses in hiding somewhere and gone on foot. But there was that saddle-tramp behind! He could quite easily be a horse-thief too, who might take a fancy to one of their nags and run the other two off, leaving them stranded. This possibility was not pleasant to think about. They would be at the mercy of the blazing sun and with miles of mighty rough territory between themselves and town, the prey of any mounted owlhooter who wanted to pick them off, leave their carcases to the buzzards. Already the usual pair of these birds of prey wheeled above them in the yellow sky. They followed anything human in these wastes, waiting patiently, hoping that somehow these creatures might be delivered to their ravenous beaks.

In any case, these three men, the young one, the old ones, had spent their lives in the saddle. They were not walking men: and their boots had certainly not been made for walking in.

'Seems to me the only thing we can do is wait for that stranger,' said Rabby at length.

'An' what do we do when he catches up with us?' asked Jim.

'We just bid him 'Howdy' and let him by.'

'We got plenty time for a smoke then.' Jim dismounted from his horse and made for some shelter from the broiling sun. Up above the vultures uttered their shrill horrible cries. There were two more of the birds further on in the sky and now Rabby pointed these out. They were probably hovering above that saddletramp, keeping pace with his slow progress without seeming to do so. That was the damnable thing about buzzards, they never seemed to move in anything but circles but they were always with you. Every time you looked up, there they were right above you, hovering as if suspended from invisible strings.

Rabby and Nevada followed Jim's example. Pretty soon they were all seated at the base of a cluster of rocks. Jim passed the 'makings' around and they lit up. The horses, relieved of their burdens, sought meagre shade too.

'Look kind a peeved don't they?' remarked Nevada. 'No grass hereabouts.'

'Hosses are like people,' said Rabby, the old wrangler. 'Though most of 'em are better than most people. Present company excepted o' course.'

'Back at the ranch they allus say Rabby likes hosses better than people,' Jim told Nevada.

'As I remember he's allus been like that,' said the old prospector. 'An' most times I'm inclined to agree with him. I guess that in my long life I've spent more time with animals than with people. I had a burro once called Joe. He was almost human. He busted a leg an' I had to shoot him. I felt like I was murdering my best friend. I cried like a baby.'

Nevada turned to his old friend. 'Remember that golden palomino you had in the old days, Rabby?' The old wrangler leaned back, closing his eyes against the sun's glare. He might have been lost in the dim past. The blue smoke from his cigarette curled lazily upwards in the still air. He said:

'I'll never forget that one. Nevady. There was a handsome piece of horseflesh! I'd never seen the like of him before, an' I've never seen his like since, nor ain't likely to.'

He turned to Jim. 'That was down in the Panhandle country. I won the horse in a game of poker. It belonged to a gambler who was down on his luck. I hated to take the beast off him. But at least I was able to assure him that I'd look after it as well as he had done.'

'What happened to the hoss?'

When he spoke again Rabby's voice was like ice. 'It got shot. We had a run-in with some drunken cow-hands . . . '

'Nesters,' put in Nevada.

'Yeh, you're right. They lived like pigs and hadn't got above a few dozen head of beef between them an' they thought we wanted to steal these . . . '

'We wouldn't have taken 'em as a gift — with the fellows' wives thrown in for makeweight . . . '

'Durn yuh,' spluttered Rabby. 'Will yuh let me tell the story my own way?'

Then his voice became grave again. 'One of the skunks drew on me an' I had to plug him in the shoulder. Then we had to run for it — we were outnumbered. One of 'em had a rifle an' he used it. He got my horse in the back o' the head, only missed me by a breath. I got up behind Nevady. We only just managed to get away. The palomino was dead o' course. We didn't even get a chance to give him a decent burial . . . '

Rabby lapsed into silence, his monkey-like face reflecting all the woes of the world. Watching him, Jim realized that there were so many facets of his old mentor's character that he barely knew, even after all the years, so much in Rabby's past that he could never share.

Here in these two men who sat with him now were the two parts of Rabby Buckthorne's life, the old and the new: Nevada and Jim. And, although these two men, the young and the old, did not know it, Rabby was reflecting that through his life he had been fortunate in his friends. Right now it seemed like he had everything. A good horse and a couple of good friends: what more could a man want?

But a man had to protect his friends. Jim was a reckless young hellion and, like so many of his generation, thought he was immortal. Nevada was so old he was past caring: he was living on borrowed time, he had said: he didn't give a damn for caution. Neither of these two had bothered to look back since they had sat down. They had lit up again and were sitting there smoking as if they were kids lying in the hay in a peaceful field. Rabby raised himself a little and looked around and over the rocks.

He did a bit of craning and contorting but he did not spot the saddle-tramp who had seemed to be following them. Probably he had not been following them at all but had spotted them and had done a little speculating himself. And had decided that as he was outnumbered and those three ginks in front might be hardcases who'd freeze a man for his boots he'd better make some kind of a detour. Rabby wished he knew for sure what the man had done. He could be hidden in the bend of the trail — if it could be called a trail. He could be hiding somewhere.

The two pairs of buzzards still wheeled up above and from time to time gave vent to their feelings of frustration. But distances were deceptive — particularly up there in the glaring cloudless sky — and the birds were of little help to Rabby. The pair that were furthest away could still be watching the stranger, but they did little to give his position away.

Rabby stayed where he was for a bit but the man did not come into sight. Nevada and Jim were silent, probably waiting for Rabby to say something.

Rabby said nothing. And, as things turned out, though he was cautious, he was not quite cautious enough. Or, at least he was cautious in the wrong direction.

10

The three men came out of the rocks facing Jim and Nevada.

They already had their guns levelled, so even if the seated men had tried anything they would not have stood a chance. All they could do was lift their hands when they were told to do so. And Rabby, turning now, did the same. And he spoke the name of the leader so that Jim, who had not seen him before, was able to identify him.

With him was his sidekick, Ponch Bates, whom Jim *had* seen before. And three more of the band, strangers to the three trapped men.

So this was Ben Jagar, thought Jim Raine, with hate and frustration.

Jagar was a big man but every part of him seemed to be somehow out of proportion. His head was freakishly enormous beneath its conventional wide-brimmed sombrero from which long black hair escaped in lank greasy snakes. His neck was bull-like, which made his sloping shoulders seem narrower than they actually were. It was as if the shoulders were pulled down by the enormous weight of the womanish chest and the pendulous stomach. There was too much chest and stomach and by contrast the legs were short and trunk-like in their tight Mexican trousers while the arms were long ape-arms. One huge hand dangled, the other held a gun, while Ben's huge face twisted into what Jim took to be a mocking smile.

Jim wanted to rush at the man, disdaining the guns, smash his fists into that leering dark face. Then get his fingers around that thick neck and choke the life out of the man who had murdered his brother. But he was not even on his feet. He and his two pards were trapped like ducks with their feet fixed in mud and the hunter only a few yards away. Ben Jagar looked like a particularly cruel and predatory hunter. He had little eyes strangely pale in so swarthy a man. He had a hook nose flattened at the end as if from a blow with a hammer. He had a wide mouth full of yellow teeth. His jowls were pendulous and he had more than one chin. He was no longer young. He wore no face adornment like so many of his contemporaries did. But he had not had a shave for some time and his beard had spread to meet the lank hair and the thick tufted eyebrows which made his appearance more ape-like than ever.

If there was any real conception of the difference between good and evil in this lawless land, Ben Jagar looked what he was: a completely evil man.

'You can rise to your feet, my friends,' he said.

His voice was not as deep as might have been expected. It was almost gentle, almost womanish. Yet, somehow, it was wholly evil too. He spoke good American with no trace of an accent.

Rabby was already standing. And

now Jim and Nevada rose slowly to their feet. Faced by a battery of levelled guns, they could not possibly make any kind of play. Neither of the three men wasted their breath by cursing these skunks who had trapped them. As they saw things now, they hadn't a Chinaman's chance. But they knew, and Ben Jagar knew, that if they saw the slightest chance of getting an edge they would take it. A fighting man could do no less.

Ben's free hand went into the pocket of his scuffed leather vest and he took out a small handful of coins which shone in the sun. Plugged pesos. He jingled them softly and winked and leered. Evidently he meant to be extravagant with them this time.

'Unbuckle your gunbelts, my friends,' he said.

'So you're just goin' to murder us, huh?' jeered Jim Raine suddenly. 'You're not going to give us any kind of chance! Ben Jagar, the fearless lobo, the wolf of the border — I've heard so much about him. I didn't think he was just a cowardly cur like the rest of the border scum. I've heard of Ben Jagar and his plugged pesos. I'd heard that he always gave a man an even break before killing him an' decorating his body with one o' these pesos . . . '

Rabby Buckthorne realized that Jim was trying the same game on Jagar as he had done on Don Ramiez's younger brother. With that vain high-born Mex it had worked, and the young man had paid for his vanity with his life. But Rabby did not think the trick was going to work this time. Ben Jagar was no high-born brother of a fabulous Don. He was fabulous in a different way and definitely did not have highfalutin ideas about honour and suchlike. But at least it was holding Ben off for a bit. He was grinning at Jim like a cat about to play with a particularly juicy mouse.

. . . And suddenly Rabby got scared, got deathly scared for Jim . . . Yes, death was one thing; probably Ben had just planned to mow them down and leave their bodies for the buzzards; but now, judging by the way he was looking at Jim after the young man's outburst, he was having other thoughts. An ear shot off perhaps to prove that the wolf was still a crackshot. A shoulder smashed, a bullet in the belly, a slow death for Jim, for all three of them. Ben was part Indian; he might be thinking up even more elaborate tortures. Had they escaped from Don Ramiez's ghouls only to fall into the hands of some even worse? And Nevada who needn't have been here at all: what a way for him to finish his long life!

They had not unbuckled their gun-belts, had been waiting it seemed for the reaction to Jim's outburst. And, for a moment, Ben Jagar seemed to forget what he had told them, and now he transferred his baleful gaze to Rabby.

And Rabby's fears were justified when Ben said: 'On second thoughts I think something special is better for my old friend Buckthorne and his friends . . . '

'Talks real purty don't he?' jeered Jim

Raine. 'A real eddicated ape. Though I didn't know apes could talk . . . '

Stop it, Jim! Rabby wanted to say. But the words would not leave his lips and Jim went on:

' . . . He ain't got the guts of an ape. He ain't got the guts of a mouse. His mother was a pig and his father was a jackal . . . '

It was the kind of cussing that white men used to inflame Indians to frothing combat. But Ben did not seem to hear them. He continued to leer at all and sundry and only his strange pale eyes were calculating and Rabby knew that he was planning what he would do to Jim, to all three of them, to Rabby Buckthorne, his old enemy and to Rabby Buckthorne's friends.

Jim cursed Ben softly and viciously in both English and bastardized Spanish when the curses sounded better that way. But Ben broke in, raising his voice for the first time, and grinning more than ever. 'It's a pity my friend Pablo Ramiez isn't here. He would enjoy this.

150

If you don't take your gunbelts off by the time I've counted three you will each have a knee smashed by a slug.'

'Better do as he says, boys,' said old Nevada, sounding as if he did not care either way.

'You got into the wrong camp, old-timer,' Ben told him. 'A foolish thing to do at your time of life.'

By this time all three men were unbuckling their gunbelts. They wanted to keep their legs intact as long as possible. They took their time over the job, for Ben had not yet started to count. Consequently, their belts had not completely fallen when Marshal Cromer of Pinto Gap rode out of hiding and, a gun in each hand, started shooting.

★   ★   ★

It was all so unexpected that everybody was taken completely by surprise.

The bandits were the most surprised, for the marshal's fire was directed at them. Also it was probable that, all the time, the other three men had had at the back of their minds a remembrance of the man they had spotted behind them a while back — though hardly in their wildest imaginings would they have thought it was the drink-sodden peace officer.

He was not too drunk now to shoot straight. He missed Ben Jager because the leader was already moving. His reflexes were faster than those of his men. Ponch Bates' gun did a graceful parobola and hit the rocks. Ponch screamed and clutched at his shoulder. Blood spouted through his tight fingers. One of the others was knocked flat on his back by a bullet that slammed into his chest. He lay still.

The clearing in the rocks beneath the blinding sun became a shambles. Rabby, Nevada and Jim had grabbed their guns too, though they had to let the unbuckled belts fall. The bandits' fire had been turned away from them. The men were instinctively potting at the mounted man who had surprised them so greatly. Only Jim Raine's eyes, in their hate, remained riveted on the face of Ben Jagar.

Jim's eyes were on Jagar as Jim went for his gun. Ben moved at the same time, dodging the marshal's first shot. He realized his danger from Jim at the same time and swivelled his gun. Jim's bullet seared his shoulder and he dropped the gun. He bounded backwards — he moved with the ungainly agility of an ape; the falling body of one of his men deflected the aim of Ben's would-be killer. And the next moment Ben was in the cover of the rocks.

Marshal Cromer tumbled from the saddle and his horse squealed with terror and bolted. The three partners were still out-numbered. 'Take cover!' yelled Rabby and grabbed Jim's arm. He almost dragged the young man into the shelter of the rocks.

One of Jagar's men lay dead. Ponch Bates had dragged himself and his wounded shoulder into cover with his chief and the other three hard-cases. By now the three men on the other side were well-covered.

They could see the body of Marshal Cromer sprawled at the left of them. Most of his face had been smashed by a heavy slug and he must have died instantly. He had made his crazy bid. It was a great pity it had ended this way. Nobody had time to conjecture now just why he had made that bid after years of drink-sodden and cowardly inactivity.

The shooting match went on. Jim Raine had managed to take his gunbelt into cover with him. But Rabby and Nevada had not been so lucky. As soon as they had emptied their guns they had to have shells from their young companion. And these would not last for ever. The other gunbelts lay in the centre of the small clearing under the burning sun. To try and reach them would mean certain death from the guns of Jagar and his men on the other side.

Shooting became desultory. There was little to shoot at, for both parties kept well in cover. Ponch Bates could be heard moaning from time to time with his busted shoulder. Flies began to buzz over the bodies of Marshal Cromer and the bandit in the clearing. Where there had been two buzzards high above in the hot sky now there were half-a-dozen or more and they were coming lower all the time, uttering their querulous cries.

The partners' horses were behind them and, luckily, out of the line of fire. And although the shooting made them skittish they were too well-tethered to be able to break away.

Rabby said: 'Ben's bound to have more men here in the hills an' the shooting will surely bring them. We're liable to get cut off. I vote we make a run for it while we still have a chance. There'll be another day.'

Even Jim saw the wisdom of this proposal. Nevada, who could wriggle on his belly like an Indian when need be, got to the horses and untied them and held them. The other two kept up a withering fire at the rocks opposite so that none of the bandits dare show their heads.

First Rabby made a run for it while Jim kept him covered. Then Jim followed.

They had mounted and were clattering away down the rocky slopes before the other side realized they had been tricked.

Bullets zipped perilously close. But neither of the partners was hit.

Their haste was communicated to the beasts they rode and on top of the shooting and the smell of blood and death, really terrified them. Where ordinarily they would have picked their way gingerly, they went down those perilous slopes now as if all the demons of Hades were at their heels. A few times one or the other of their three riders were almost unseated but, cursing and swaying, managed to hang on. And, in a surprisingly short space of time they reached comparatively level ground. Then the sparse grass of the plain — and on to Pinto Gap.

When they reached the town the sun was going in. Nobody seemed to notice their return with any great interest. Earlier red-headed Sal had told them of a livery-stable nearer to the one they had used before. Kept by an American, it was the place which she recommended all her horse-riding visitors.

The American owner proved to be a little elderly man with a pegleg and small birdlike eyes. When they told him Sal had sent them he shook them all warmly by the hand and said any friends of Sal's were friends of his.

They figured their horses would be better in his hands than in the hands of the shifty Mexican they had hired the day before. Besides, that greaser could quite easily be in the pay of the other side. It seemed to them that two-thirds of the population of Pinto Gap could quite easily belong to what they could not help but think of as 'the other side'.

The partners seemed to be fighting their own private war. They could not contemplate the possibility of getting any reinforcements to 'their side' in this hellhole.

However, Rabby Buckthorne voted they went back into the hills at the dead of night and brought in Marshal Cromer's body, or what was left of it. That was the least they could do for this strange man who had, in effect, saved their lives. They might be able to get his and Nevada's gunbelts back too, if Ben Jagar's men happened to overlook them.

Jim and Nevada could not say no to this proposal any more than they could to most of Rabby's proposals. They knew they were taking a big risk in going back into enemy territory so soon like this. It was doubtful whether Ben Jagar would be expecting them anyway; they might get a measure of sardonic amusement out of the trip to make up for the loss of sleep.

Jim said that next time they made a

sortie into the hills looking for skunks they ought to go by night anyway. The other two agreed. But first to get the marshal's body in.

On their way to the lodging house they agreed that nothing of their afternoon's adventure should be told to the people there, not even to Sal.

What did they know about red-headed Sal — or anybody else in that house — after all?

11

There was a moon and that was not good for their purpose. They took a chance anyway. They rode hard across the yellow plain. The Crackerjacks were like animals crouching, waiting. They forced their horses up the slopes, but left them tethered at a lower point than they had earlier that day.

They went the rest of the way on foot, half-crouching most of the time. The noise they made sounded terribly loud to them in the stillness. There was no wind. The moonlight was piteous.

All of them, in their separate ways, began to think they might have made a mistake, coming out like this. In a way, this was a very quixotic gesture, coming out to fetch a dead body, risking their lives to do so. The man had saved their lives. But had he really meant to save their lives? Why had he been following them? If he had been following them!

There was a mystery in rumpot Cromer suddenly turning into a fighting man, dying a fighting man. Perhaps bringing back the body would in some way help to solve that mystery. Cromer might have spoken to somebody in town before he left . . .

There were the two gun-belts as well, of course. They were good gun-belts. At least, their aged owners thought they were. Rabby's, for instance, was a new one. He had only just bought it to replace the one he had left behind at the rancho of Don Ramiez.

Rabby and Nevada carried their guns now in the waistbands of their trousers. Jim was ahead of them. They kept a distance between them, covering the hotheaded younker. He stopped suddenly and they thought he had heard something or seen something. Then he waved them on, and catching him up, they realized they had reached their journey's end.

Marshal Cromer's body was still

there. The buzzards had been at it.

The feathered buzzards had made a mess; they did not know any better. But human buzzards had stripped the body of all useable accoutrements, even to the boots and hat. Rabby and Nevada's gun-belts had vanished too.

'We might have known,' said Nevada in a hoarse whisper. 'You know what these peons are. They'd rob their own mother of her teeth before they dropped her in her grave.'

They made a lot more noise getting the body back down to the horses. But nothing happened. Ben Jagar evidently had not bothered to leave a look-out. Doubtless the bandit camp was much further back in the hills.

Nevada's horse was the oldest and largest, a rawboned giant. He jittered a little as the body was placed across his back. Nevada gentled him with his hands and soft cajoling voice. Like his pard, Rabby, this oldster too had spent more time with animals than human beings. He understood the dumb beasts and they trusted him. He covered the body with an old piece of tarp he had brought along for that purpose. He mounted behind it.

Both Rabby and he could remember the nights in the old days when they had been fighting Indians and had fetched in the mutilated corpses of their comrades.

Nevada said: 'I ought to've got them two burros o' mine. One of 'em would've done fine for a job like this to save putting the burden on ol' Mose here. He's a mighty sensitive cayuse is ol' Mose.'

'He looks it,' chuckled Rabby. 'Lookit those big soulful eyes. Loading him down with a body has hurt his feelings terribly.'

'He'll get over it.'

'I hope those burros o' yourn are all right.'

'Yeh, I left 'em food — and there's water there. They'll be all right, unless somebody comes an' runs them off. I guess I oughta get rid of 'em now I ain't gonna do any more prospecting.'

'You really set about that, Nevady? Not doing any more prospecting I mean.'

'Yeh. Way I feel right now it's as if I've wasted a lot o' years grubbing about in the back o' beyond, hidin' myself away from my own kind like a gopher diggin' funkholes to hell an' back . . . I'm even enjoying this . . . ' He made a gesture encompassing the moon-washed plain, his two pards, even the carcase on the front of his saddle. The smell of this was in his nostrils, but even that was part of this new adventure, this reliving (in his old age) of an old adventure with 'young Rabby Buckthorne'.

'It's like old times,' he said.

There was silence for a few moments. Then Rabby said: 'You said you'd sell your burros an' tackle to that Mex at the livery stables.'

'I don't trust that greaser now,' said Nevada. 'But how about that little fellow we leave the hosses with now?

Big Sal recommended him highly. Remind me to speak to him about the burros will yuh — my memory ain't as good as it useter be.'

'Sure. I dessay he'll be glad to take 'em off your hands.'

'They're mighty fine burros . . . '

'Gab, gab, gab,' cut in Jim Raine. 'I do declare you two are like a couple of old women.'

There was underlying mirth in his deep voice. His white teeth flashed. Looking at him, Rabby thought the younker was coming out of his savage brooding mood. Not that that made him any the less dangerous. Cooler, if anything.

Dawn was parting the sky when the three partners and their silent companion got back to Pinto Gap.

The town was asleep. But heads began to appear tentatively at windows as the three horses clopped down the main drag, awakening the echoes.

They drew up outside the livery stable kept by Sal's little old friend. He must have heard them. He opened the side door.

They told him the marshal had got himself shot doing his duty. If the livery-man seemed to find anything strange in this he did not say so. He did not ask questions. These weren't the kind of men you asked questions of — particularly the young one. Besides, they were friends of Sal's. They asked him where the undertaking parlour was and he directed them.

The undertaker, a man with his wall-eye well on the main chance, was already out of bed. When they knocked he yelled, 'All right. I'm coming.'

He opened the door and they carried the body into the place and put it on a trestle. The undertaker's half-voiced questions died in his prim mouth. The young man with the hot threatening eyes said, 'We're staying at Sal's place if anybody needs us.' Then they left.

They went back to the livery stable to leave their horses. Rabby reminded Nevada to ask about the burros.

Nevada did so and the little man said he'd be glad to take the beasts off his hands in the morning. Everybody said 'Goodnight'. (Good morning!). Everybody went to bed.

Sal was heard to peep out of her room. But she didn't say anything. Jim Raine noted that the lock was still broken on the door of the big woman's room. He wondered why she had not mentioned it. Maybe she had something up her sleeve in connection with it.

* * *

They slept late the following morning and, when they got down to breakfast, all the other lodgers had left.

They told Sal about the death of Marshal Cromer.

She said: 'I guess that was the way he'd have wanted to go after all. He was a good lawman once.'

She went back into the kitchen and Rabby, addressing his partners, said:

'We didn't go through Cromer's pockets. We ought've done, even though it would be an unpleasant job.'

'I guess we figured Ben's boys would have picked him clean,' said Nevada.

Jim said: 'We'll go down to the undertaking parlour. I didn't like the look o' that galoot there anyway. He looked as if he would be capable of filching a dead man's teeth.'

They finished their breakfast right after and walked down to the undertaker's. He was still in bed. They hammered the door until he came down and let them in. They did not tell him what they wanted, just walked in, got in a huddle round the body.

All they found was a folded blood-stained paper in a vest pocket.

But it was interesting.

It was a reward poster.

It had come from another part of the West and offered five hundred dollars for the capture of Ben Jagar, dead or alive.

'So Cromer was only bounty-hunting

after all,' said Jim Raine disgustedly.

'Looks that way,' agreed Rabby Buckthorne. 'This looks like quite an old dodger. Cromer had probably been hogging it for some time, dreaming, wondering how he could get Ben without being shot up by Ben or his men. Cromer must've known we were after Ben — things get around in a town like this. So Cromer took a chance with us, followed us like a jackal following a mountain lion, ready to pick over the bones after the kill. He thought we might lead him to Ben an' he could step in somehow an' claim the reward. Mebbe I'm misjudging the man an' speaking very ill of the dead, as the saying goes. But that's the way it looks ain't it?'

'Suttinly is,' said Nevada.

'I wonder,' said Rabby, 'if he had a kind of change of heart — at the last I mean. The way he came out of hiding and started blasting, the odds all against him an' all, was certainly somethin'.'

169

'It was,' said Jim. 'Yeh, it was.'

'Then that's the way we gotta think about it,' said Rabby. ' 'Cos, no matter which way you look at it, if it wasn't for this poor crittur lying here we wouldn't be standing here right now.' He put the reward bill solemnly into his pocket. 'That's the way we'll be telling it,' he said.

The other two nodded. The three of them grunted curt So-longs to the undertaker. Then they left the place.

People stared at them curiously as they walked along the street. Some of these had seen them ride into town at dawn with the body over the saddle. Now they knew it had been Marshal Cromer's body they had seen. Almost everybody knew this by now. The news had travelled fast. But they did not know the all of it and everybody was leary of asking the first question.

The partners went to the livery-stable and got their horses. Then they rode out to where they had left Nevada's burros. This was in a tiny natural amphitheatre in the centre of which a tiny spring bubbled from the ground, though there was no sign of water elsewhere in the vicinity, this being right on the edge of the badlands.

Nevada said he had spent lazy days here time back and had not seen hide nor hair of man or beast, except his own animals that he had brought with him. It was in fact one of his own animals, a burro, that had led him here in the first place. They might be ugly little beasts but they had noses as sharp as all get-out . . . Nevada went into raptures again in his praise of burros. Jim told him *they* weren't buying any spavined critturs with big ears, to save his spiel for the livery-man.

They were good burros though; the livery-man admitted this when they got them back to Pinto Gap. He gave Nevada quite a good price for them, and for the prospecting gear that went with them.

So old Nevada cut himself away completely from his old life.

They went to have a drink to kind of celebrate this.

There were not many people in The Don Amigo. Jim, Nevada and Rabby were given plenty of room at the bar. Now was the chance for the wiseacres to ask questions if they wanted to. The partners did not get too close together. They took their drinks and they leaned their elbows on the bar and half-turned. Between them they could watch every sector of the room.

Both Rabby and Nevada were minus gunbelts. They still had their guns tucked into the waist-bands of their trousers, and were somewhat peeved by this. They were used to having their gun-butts much lower than this, so they could reach them for a quick draw without being slowed up with a lot of elbow-bending. A lot of elbow-bending could mean the difference between a man's life and his death. That was a helluva lot of difference. Rabby said he aimed to go and get himself a new gunbelt as soon as he'd had his fill of liquor. Nevada said: him too! They did not anticipate any trouble from the mealy-mouthed lot of characters that were in the saloon now. Still, you never knew!

Jim Raine stood with one elbow on the bar and that hand idly playing with his glass of liquor. His other hand was near to the butt of his gun in its low-slung holster.

When he started out with Rabby after leaving the KP boys with their burden of grief he had worn an old rig he had gotten used to. But he had lost this when he escaped from the Ramiez Rancho and, like Rabby, had had to buy a new rig. He missed his old rig but he had practised with this new one and figured he could manage pretty fair if he had to.

'Hell,' groaned Rabby. 'All I seem to be doing lately is buy gunbelts. Lookit all the hooch I could buy with the money I'm spending on gunbelts. That's somep'n else that Ben Jagar — yeh, an' Pablo Ramiez too — have got to answer for.'

'Yuh durn tootin',' said Nevada.

'What you moaning about? You've only lost one gunbelt. I've lost two gunbelts — an' one damn' fine gun on top o' that. Not to mention my ol' Sharps gun. Hell, I've had that ol' Sharps . . . '

'If it's that ol' Sharps you had when I knew you last it ain't much loss. I'm surprised you ain't blown yourself up with it by now.'

Rabby grinned widely. 'Come to think of it, I almost did. With that ol' Sharps you mentioned I mean. A real mean gun. It seemed to have a grudge agin me. Barrel blew apart for no reason at all. Took my eyebrows an' part o' my hair.'

Nevada guffawed. 'I allus knew that gun would turn loco in the end.'

'Guns are kinda like people and hosses ain't they?' said Nevada. 'Only more like people than hosses I guess — kinda treacherous sometimes. I bought me another Sharps in place o' that one. Looked jest like the first one. But a different temperament altogether . . . '

'Watch yourself with them big words.'

'The sweetest-tempered gun I ever handled . . . Still, whichever o' those Ramiez boys have got it now, I hope it turns on him an' blows him to Kingdom Come . . . '

'Gab, gab, gab,' said Jim Raine automatically. He downed his second drink and, as it was his turn to pay, called for three refills.

He knocked his third one back quickly. He shuddered. 'Even the likker don't taste right somehow. C'mon, let's get out of this place. These goo-goo-eyed people are giving me a pain in the neck.'

He did not bother to lower his voice and there was no doubt some of the bystanders heard what he said. Jim seemed to be spoiling for a fight, reflected Rabby; maybe it would be better if they quit this place pronto.

He downed his drink. He nudged

Nevada. 'C'mon old-timer.'

Nevada drained the dregs in his glass, grimaced. The three men made for the door. Jim looked about him arrogantly as if daring anybody to ask their questions while they still had the chance, before their quarry passed through the doors.

Things were not going fast enough for Jim. Somebody here might be able to tell him where Ben Jagar was hiding out now. How anybody could, he did not know; it was just that frustration was eating at him again and he would have welcomed a move from somebody, anybody.

Maybe he just wanted a rough-house in order to relieve his feelings. He wasn't sure what he did want — except, of course, to avenge his brother's death. He only knew he hated this town and all the scum that hung around it and all these mealy-mouthed characters who tolerated the scum because, like the parasites they were, they lived off it.

He would like to take this saloon apart!

He would like to take the town apart!

But nobody let out a peep, nobody gave him a chance to get started. And he and his two partners passed through and the batwings swung to behind them.

Baleful glances were flung at the gently-swinging batwings. More than one person in the saloon wished they could take that arrogant young puppy down a peg or two. And they would too if they had half a chance. As long as they didn't have to face his guns or his fists, of course: he looked as lean and mean and strong and fast as a lobo wolf.

Meanwhile the three partners went on to the gunsmith's and Rabby and Nevada got themselves fixed up with a new rig. Then they went back to Sal's for a meal.

12

The moonlight streamed into the room. The three men had not had much sleep the night before and were making it up now. Rabby and Nevada both snored. They had kept Jim awake for a while and once or twice he had been on the verge of yelling at them to turn over or something. But it seemed such a shame to wake the two old coots. He dozed and wrestled with his thoughts, and finally he fell asleep. Although he did not realize it, he snored himself. He slept deeply.

The window was closed. But they had not locked the door. What were they, kids to be scared of shadows and bogey-men? Nevada had said they ought to put piles of crumpled paper round their beds like Wild Bill Hickok used to, so he could hear anybody who tried to creep up on him during the night. But they hadn't any paper and were too tired to be fooling around. So they laughed at the old prospector's sense of humour and settled down.

Afterwards they realized how foolhardy they had been. They might at least have locked the door!

They were sleeping too deeply to hear the door opening. The first inkling Jim Raine had of any danger was when a gun was poked into his ribs and a voice said, 'Take it gently now.'

He awoke quickly and froze. The hard muzzle grinding into his flesh was unmistakable. Slowly he sat up. He realized that his own weapon was no longer there. The hold-up man had taken the gun away from Jim's side and had straightened up. Jim saw the shine of two guns, one in each of the man's fists. One of them was probably Jim's own gun.

There were more men over by the larger bed on which Rabby and Nevada slept. The room seemed full of men. Jim could hear his two partners grunting and expostulating as they awoke. Being older, they weren't so quick on the uptake as him.

And he had been damned slow. He cursed himself silently. He looked up at the man above him, the nebulous white mass of face.

'Who are you?'

The man did not answer but another voice did. 'Light the lamp, one of you — then the young man can see us all.'

This voice sounded familiar. It was undeniably Mexican. But it had no thick accent. It was what you might call a cultured Mexican voice. And even as the lamplight blossomed, Jim guessed who the man was.

He stood in the centre of the floor, the intrepid General. The tall, lean, stooped man with the long thick iron-grey hair escaping from beneath the beautiful sombrero. With the hawk-like face brown and wrinkled as old leather. With the cruel black eyes and the thin imperious lips.

'Hell, it's Pablo Ramiez,' said Rabby

Buckthorne with disgust.

There were six men, including Don Ramiez. Only another one of them was a Mexican and the partners did not recognize him. Probably an aide-de-camp the Don had brought with him from the rancho. He was the youngest man there, with the exception of Jim. The other four men were Americans. They were middle-aged and at least two of them had pot-bellies. Although they each held a gun, none of them wore gunbelts. Jim Raine had an idea he had seen one or two of them around town. That little fat character with a squint, for instance: surely he had been in the saloon this afternoon.

'Get out and stand beside your beds,' snapped Ramiez.

The man covering Jim had stepped back a little. He was heavy-set but did look a little more dangerous than the other pot-bellies, storekeepers or whatever they were. The other gun he held was indeed Jim's. He jerked this. 'Do as you're told, son,' he said.

Jim did as he was told, noting that Rabby and Nevada were doing that too. There was little else they could do. They looked old and rather foolish in their baggy union underwear. Jim knew he looked no fashion-plate himself.

He was seized by a sudden spasm of fury. 'All right, cut the play-acting,' he yelled. 'What do you want with us?'

'Keep your voice low,' snarled Ramiez. He had a temper too. He was a nasty old sidewinder.

'You oughta know what the bloody-minded old villain wants with us, Jim,' said Rabby.

'All greasers are bloody-minded back-shooting skunks,' said Nevada mildly. How beautifully those two old goats play along, thought Jim.

But Ramiez was not to be drawn. He said: 'We are the Pinto Gap Vigilantes . . . '

Jim Raine broke into raucous laughter. The heavy-set man lashed out with one of the guns. Jim stepped back just in time, the barrel of the gun barely missed his temple.

'Hold it,' said Ramiez. He looked at the heavy-set man. 'If he tries any more tricks, just shoot him. We are in our rights here. Shoot him for resisting arrest.'

'Ain't you boys got some nice shiny badges you can wear?' asked Rabby.

Ramiez ignored him; said, 'This is a citizens' vigilante committee that has been formed . . . '

'Hell, you don't even live here . . . '

' . . . that has been formed because of the sudden demise of Marshal Cromer. It will continue to function until another marshal is sent to take Cromer's place . . . '

'Who do you think you're fooling? As long as you have anything to do with it, there won't be another marshal.' Rabby Buckthorne's head wagged around to the other men. 'Are you letting this old greaser faze you? Don't you see that he'll take over your town? Him and his boys an' those of his bosom friend, Ben Jagar, will turn the place into a bigger hell-hole than it was before. I tell you . . .'

The rest of Rabby's words were choked off in a groan. Ramiez had moved with tigerish swiftness. His gun whipped across and the barrel was laid with a dull thud against Rabby's temple. Rabby hit the side of the bed, slid to the floor, lay still.

His face white with passion, Jim started forward. But he stopped at the threat of murder in the eyes of the heavy-set man in front of him. To get himself shot in the belly would not help Rabby at all. He looked past the two guns, looked at Ramiez.

'Some day,' he said clearly and distinctly, 'I'm going to kill you.'

Nevada said quietly, 'Not if I see him first.' Disregarding the guns, the old prospector bent over his fallen friend.

'Where you're going you won't have a chance to kill anybody else,' said Ramiez.

'What do you mean by that?' demanded Jim Raine.

184

'We're taking you in for the murder of Marshal Cromer.'

Jim laughed sardonically, 'So that's it!'

'I don't think it's very funny,' said Nevada. 'If they think they can get away . . . '

He broke off, bent nearer to Rabby, who had begun to groan. Rabby opened his eyes, began to rise. There was a great swelling welt across his temple but the skin was not broken. As Nevada helped him to his feet, Rabby's gaze became fixed on Pablo Ramiez. Jim Raine had never seen such an expression in his old friend's eyes before. Here was another man who wanted to kill the suave, cruel Don.

'Let's take them down to the jail,' said Ramiez.

'Are you men going to let him fool you?' asked old Nevada.

'He's not fooling us,' said the heavy-set man who covered Jim. 'You're the ones who tried to fool us. Bringing in Cromer's body yourself an' telling a cock-and-bull story about him being shot by bandits in the hill — that wouldn't fool a child. Some mighty queer things have happened in this town since you three bozos turned up. Cromer was seen to ride out after you, tailing you. We think he'd got something on you and you killed him to keep his mouth shut. Don Ramiez has already told us how you were caught rustling his cattle an' you killed his younger brother. You'll be glad to tell us the whole tale before we've finished with you . . . '

'I can imagine,' said Jim Raine. 'No doubt you're a dandy man with a hot iron.' He had just remembered where he had seen this fellow before. He was the town blacksmith. No doubt he got a lot of work from the Ramiez rancho.

Jim went on, lashing them with his tongue: 'You all dicker with Ramiez don't you? You might lose a few precious dollars if he turns his back on you mightn't you? You know he's a thief an' a rustler and a murderer. You know he's hand in glove with Ben Jagar and he hates us Americans an' all we stand for worse than poison. But you don't mind all this as long as you can fill your greedy craws with money. You're the biggest measliest bunch of coyote whelps I've seen in my life. As for this man,' disregarding the guns, he stabbed a finger at Ramiez, 'can't you see that he's so eaten up with hate and lust for power that he ain't sane any more.'

Ramiez came at him then — looking like a madman. Almost knocking the heavy-set man over in his haste. His gun was pointing at Jim's stomach when the door burst open.

Ramiez whirled; everybody whirled, guns lifting.

Ponch Bates staggered into the room. His arm was in a black sling. There was blood on his face. Behind him were Sal and a shotgun; and old Calhoun who had a revolver in each hand.

Jim Raine swung. His fist caught Ramiez on the angle of the jaw and the Mexican went down, his gun leaving his hand and skittering along the floor. The window smashed and the barrel of a rifle was poked through. Behind it was the white heart-shaped face of Ella Calhoun.

Taken on all sides, their leader wallowing dazedly on the floor, the 'vigilantes' were utterly demoralized.

'Drop your guns,' barked old Calhoun, and even the truculent blacksmith obeyed with alacrity.

Jim and his two partners collected the weapons and dropped them on to the bed, retaining their own guns. Jim opened the window and let Ella in. She must have climbed up the roof of that lean-to outside like a cat. She wore her shirt-waist and skirt but her black hair was unbound and wild around her shoulders. She looked at her father and Sal and said:

'I heard most of it from out there. This bunch — with Ramiez leading them — call themselves vigilantes. They were trying to railroad the three boys for the murder of Marshal Cromer.'

Ramiez was climbing slowly to his feet, his face white with hate, his eyes flaring demoniacally. Right then he really looked like a crazy man and even his erstwhile followers eyed him askance, hoping he wouldn't try anything foolish. Sal looked as if she would dearly love to start blasting with that shotgun. With her mass of red hair and her oversize dressing gown she looked a real wild woman.

But Ramiez wasn't crazy enough to rush those guns. He just stood, half-crouching, glaring.

'Up to your devil's tricks again are you, Pablo?' said Calhoun.

'You keep out of this.'

'Too late. We're in! And we aim to show these poor boobs,' his contemptuous gaze swept the ranks of the 'vigilantes' . . . 'the error of their reasoning.' Old Calhoun spat drily. 'You're being made suckers of, gentlemen. This town doesn't need Ramiez or any of his kind. It could be a good town if you'd stop to think about that, if you'd work a little towards that. It could be a far more prosperous town, too, with decent people coming in all the time instead of killers an' thieves who do more harm than good . . . '

Pablo Ramiez spat something out in his own tongue.

Calhoun ignored him. 'He brags about being highborn. But he's just filth. I know him better than any of you. My late wife was a relative of his. She hated him for what he was and for the bad name he had brought her family.'

Ramiez moved. Jim Raine said: 'You'll keep still, *señor*, or I'll knock you down again — an' this time with a gun-barrel.'

'No, let me do that,' said Rabby Buckthorne.

'I can endorse everything my good friend here says,' spoke up red-headed Sal rather pompously. 'Ramiez and his breed get their own people a bad name. You all remember my late husband. He was a Mexican an' some folks held that against him. But you all know he was a good man. He worked for Ramiez before he came here. You didn't know that did you? An' when he set up on his own Ramiez tried more than once to run him out. My husband hated Ramiez and all his kind . . . '

'He was a pig,' said Ramiez.

'Watch your mouth, mister. I ain't aiming to play with you. Another remark like that an' I'll fill your belly with buckshot.' Sal so obviously meant what she said. She went on: 'Why, if my husband was alive now, you wouldn't be fit to lick his boots, for all your swank an' your fancy talk an' your rancho an' all.'

Ramiez did not say anything else and, watching the man, Jim Raine sensed that at last he was getting scared. In some subtle way he was beginning to look older, an evil old man like a moulting hawk.

Old Calhoun said: 'You made a mistake in bringing Ponch Bates here along with you an' leaving him on lookout. Everybody knows Ponch is

Ben Jagar's right-hand man. If having Ponch along don't tie you up conclusively with Jagar I'd like to know what does . . . '

'Ponch got that arm in the gun-battle with the marshal,' put in Jim Raine, 'when the marshal was killed.'

'Tell 'em all about it, Ponch,' said Nevada. 'Tell 'em how the marshal was killed.'

Ponch glowered evilly and said nothing. Sal jabbed him with the muzzle of the shotgun. 'Talk little fat man,' she said.

'Go to hell, yuh big freak,' said Ponch.

Sal swung the shotgun up and sideways. The barrel slammed against the side of Ponch's head and he went down like a skittle. He yelled with pain as he jarred his wounded arm. He rolled over, looked up dazedly, fearfully, at Sal. She poked the gun muzzle downwards until it was a few inches from the man's face. Her finger whitened on the trigger.

'Who killed Marshal Cromer?'

'Ben Jagar shot him. Ben ... ' Ponch's voice cracked with terror.

Old Calhoun's peppery contemptuous gaze raked the 'vigilantes' again. 'D'yuh hear that? But you might have guessed something like that, mightn't you, if you'd stopped to think? Seeing Ramiez running with this skunk, all skunks together. But you didn't want to stop an' think did you? The customer's always right isn't he?' Calhoun's choleric turkey-face became redder than ever, his voice rose to a bellow. 'You pack of mangy curs! Call yourself men? You're nothing but a pack of jackals running with your noses to the ground to pick up the scraps ... '

'Now look ... ' began the heavy-set blacksmith lamely.

'Shet your trap! Think yourselves damned lucky I don't set Sal loose on yuh with this scatter-gun.'

'Just gimme the word, Brother Calhoun.'

'We'll take Ramiez and his two

pardners down to the jail an' lock 'em up,' said Calhoun. 'Then in the morning we'll send for a new marshal — a good one this time — an' a circuit judge. We ought to be able to get enough on Ramiez to hang him.'

'I vote we string him up right away,' said old Nevada.

'We cain't do that. We've got to have things legal.'

'Yeh, I guess you're right. Pity!'

'I think Ramiez's two pards might be able to give us something on Ramiez.' Calhoun poked a gun at Ponch and at the younger Mexican, who stood like a graven image. Only his dark eyes were alive and they were full of fear. Ponch looked on the point of cracking too.

The three prisoners were ushered out first. Ramiez now maintained a brooding silence.

The erstwhile vigilantes were not given their guns back. They filed out like sheep.

13

They were crossing in front of the house when the young Mexican made the break. He had been in the forefront. He had looked so scared that nobody had paid a lot of attention to him. He was the last person they would have expected to make a break. Maybe he hadn't understood everything that had been said. Maybe he thought they aimed to lynch him there and then out among the dark trees that reached and curled in the macabre moonlight. He must have been half-demented to take such a chance while guns bristled at his back.

His terror or his recklessness gave his feet wings. Ramiez was between old Calhoun and the fleeing man. Calhoun swore, changed his position, fired. The Mexican gave a little hoppity-skip then went on. Ramiez made a desperate grab for Calhoun's gun arm. Sal jabbed the barrel of her shotgun viciously into Ramiez's back and the man sprawled at her feet. The young Mexican had vanished in the trees.

Jim Raine said, 'I'll go after him. Don't wait for me.'

'Right, son.'

Jim ran into the trees. Ramiez was dragged to his feet and the cavalcade moved on.

'He won't get far,' said old Calhoun. 'I think I hit him.'

His daughter was at his side. She had insisted on coming along: to keep Sal company she said. She carried her rifle in the crook of her arm. She was a crack-shot. Her father had taught her. Old Calhoun knew that Ella could have fetched that Mexican down easily with her rifle but he was glad she hadn't tried.

Running through the dark trees, Jim Raine wondered whether the Mexican had been hit. The ground seemed to have opened up and swallowed him.

Maybe he had laid down somewhere already to die. Maybe he hadn't been hit at all but had only ducked and tripped when old Calhoun shot at him.

Jim stopped to listen. He could not hear a thing except the faint soughing of the wind and the diminishing sounds made by his friends back there as they went on their way. He went on again. In this small grove the trees were close together and met overhead. Jim had to dodge and swerve, going by instinct as much as anything else, for in parts the blackness was almost surrounded by underbrush and creepers, so that Jim had to climb or pick his way through.

Years ago this area had been part of a small forest and the settlers had come and cut down some of the trees and made their clearings and built their rude houses. They had not bothered to clear all the forest and shrubberies away and it remained here and there, as in this particular spot on the edge of town; it flourished, encroached in the strangest places.

Jim did not know this; he was a stranger to this part of the country. He did not know that this particular piece of thickly wooded ground was only a narrow strip; to him it seemed endless. His ears were taut for any sound; his eyes strained into the darkness. He tripped over trailing roots and branches. He had put his gun away so he could use both his hands to help himself along.

He was almost at the edge of the tangle when the thing happened; though Jim did not know he was near the edge: as far as he knew he might have been in the middle.

The young Mexican must have had time to think. He could not have been as craven as he seemed or Don Ramiez would not have picked him for his aide-de-camp. Maybe his panic had only been momentary; maybe there had been no real panic at all, maybe he was just a reckless young fool who had taken an awful chance which, so far, had paid off. Probably he realized after a time that there was only one person chasing him. But that person would surely have a gun and he himself had no gun. And when he ran out of the trees and into the bright moonlight and crossed the open space to where the horses stood he would be a perfect target for any average marksman . . .

★   ★   ★

The figure rose up beside Jim. He sensed it rather than saw it. He reached instinctively for his gun. But it would have been better if he had not. The Mexican had found a heavy branch to use as a club and Jim's hands were down, he wasn't covering himself: the weapon thumped into his head and he went down.

His attacker bent over him, reaching for the low-slung gun. Jim was dazed. But savage with himself for being caught this way. And his savagery gave him strength. He lunged upwards. His fingers scratched against flesh, found the other man's throat. The man fell on top of him, broke the hold. They grunted and scrabbled and panted in the hot foetid darkness at the foot of the trees among the clawing under-brush and the entangling creepers.

Jim used his knees as levers. He rammed a fist into a lean middle. The man rolled off him. But he still had hold of his improvised club and now he used it again. Jim felt the wind of it as it narrowly missed his face. He lunged forward desperately. He only grabbed at air. The Mexican was using his club like a flail. It smacked on Jim's right elbow, sending a jet of pain to his shoulder then momentarily numbing the arm completely.

Jim sensed the next blow instinctively and tried to cover up. The concussion was terrific. Something seemed to explode in his skull. The night spun around him, shot with blood and flashing white stars. He went back again, striving for consciousness, holding on to the last agonizing shred of it.

The young Mexican did not try for the gun this time. All he wanted to do now was to get away as quickly as possible in case the sounds of their battle had been heard. He ran, crashing through the bushes and undergrowth.

Vaguely, Jim Raine heard him go. He willed himself to follow him. He raised himself out of a treacly black morass that seemed to be trying to hold him down. He got to his knees. Then to his feet. His hand found the roughness of a tree-trunk and he held on to it for a moment; breathing, fighting the hammering at his head that threatened to sink him again. He began to move forward. He blundered into a tree and stopped, trying to orient himself.

Hoofbeats started up ahead of him, the sound becoming rapid, fading quickly. He tried to move faster. He ignored branches that whipped at his face and body, that plucked at his legs.

He broke out suddenly into the brilliant moonlight. There was no sign of the horseman. Or any more horses. It had seemed to Jim that there had been more than one horse.

He did not know that Pablo Ramiez's horse had been there too and that the young Mexican had run it off so that Jim could not follow him right away. There were no more horses near. The townsfolk members of the erstwhile vigilante party had not had far to come so they had walked.

Jim's own horse was in the stables and he would have to wake the old livery-man up in order to get it. Jim knew he could not possibly catch the fleeing man. He was so enraged with himself that he felt sick. His head hammered like something inside it was trying to beat it's way free. Jim raised his hand and felt gingerly among the matted hair. Although he had donned a modicum of civilised dress before he came out here he had not had time to comb his hair or put his hat on.

There was a nasty swelling ridge. It was gummy too; his fingers came away wet.

He oriented himself again, finding even this a little difficult to do. A little shakily — thudding head at one end, scuffed high-heeled boots at the other — he began to walk.

He found his way to the marshal's office. The lights were on. The blinds were drawn. He tried the door and found it locked. From inside a voice called, 'Who is it?'

'It's me — Jim Raine.'

The door was opened by old Calhoun. His daughter was still there too in the lamplit office. So was big Sal. And Rabby and Nevada. Pablo Ramiez and Ponch Bates were back in the cell but the rest of the erstwhile vigilantes remained in the office, though they had not yet been given their guns back.

'Hell, Jim, what happened to you?' asked Rabby.

Jim told his story. He didn't let himself down lightly. He had walked into an ambush, he said, like a kid who was still wet behind the ears.

'He'll go right back to the rancho,'

burst out one of the pot-bellied vigilantes. 'He'll get as many men as he can and they'll come back here after their boss. They won't be particular — they'll give this town hell.'

The vigilantes shuffled their feet. They were a sorry bunch of sheep now. They needed somebody else to tell them what to do.

Old Calhoun said: 'Well, if they come we'll just have to fight 'em that's all. It's time we stuck up to some o' this scum anyway. Are you with me? Or would you like to join your two pards in that cell?'

'There's no need for that,' said the heavy-set blacksmith, whose name was Brodie.

'There's nothing else we can do but fight if they come,' said another man.

'They'll come sooner or later,' said old Calhoun. Sal and Ella were inspecting Jim's head. Sal got some water boiled and Ella bathed the wound. Her fingers were long and gentle, her dark eyes intent. Stray spirals of her black hair tickled his cheek as she bent over him. She smelled nicely. Jim didn't know a heck of a lot about women; but he kind of cottoned to this one.

She rubbed some salve into his head. He'd live, he said, and she smiled at him and said she hoped so.

14

They alerted the town.

Some people thought it was some kind of a trick. There was a lot of confusion; there were a lot of recriminations, some of them among the erstwhile vigilante party; there was some near-panic.

There was no time to get proper defences together. The leaders of defence — old Calhoun was foremost among these — could only hope that when the raiders came everybody would be ready for them. What kind of a fight the townspeople would put up remained to be seen.

The folks at the law-office 'spelled' each other, taking it in turns to rest on the couch in the quarters of the late Marshal Cromer. Pablo Ramiez and Ponch Bates yelled abuse from the cell-block. They had listened to the talk and knew their young Mexican friend had escaped. They were very cocky. Ramiez said the town would be put to the fire, razed to the ground and everybody in it killed. He was like a madman as he poured out a stream of hate against the *Americanos*. Listening to him, his erstwhile partners, the American members of the 'vigilantes', realized what fools they had been.

The man was a megalomaniac. He ought to be put down like a rabid dog.

Sal and Ella went back to the lodging house to get some warmer clothes both for themselves and the men. They were going to stick at the law-office they said. There was no use arguing with them. They were both good shots, probably better than some of the men there.

The night was cold, as nights can be cold in those parts no matter how hot the day has been.

Dawn slowly crept up like a grey cat. But it brought nothing else. Did the raiders mean to attack by daylight? That hardly seemed likely.

At dawn some of the hard-cases rode away from the town, taking their meagre belongings with them. They evidently thought there was going to be a raid at some time or the other and they didn't want to be caught in the middle of it. Pinto Gap meant nothing to them, except as a refuge from the law. And now they didn't feel so safe as they had done in the past.

They would make no difference to things one way or the other, unless they joined the 'other side'.

The attack did not come. The sun rose. Pinto Gap seemed as normal and dusty as ever. Folks began to say it was a false alarm, began to go about their usual business of the day. But the party in the law-office were not fooled. They knew the raiders would come sooner or later. Probably they had been too late to come last night. But they would come. Pablo Ramiez was sure they would come. That old goat knew!

A guard was posted on a high point at each end of town. The guards were changed at intervals. There was business to be done. But the alarm could soon be given. Nevada and Rabby went with Sal back to the lodging house for breakfast. Jim said he would go by when they returned. He stayed at the office with old Calhoun and Ella.

The girl dozed on a couch. She looked very childish now, despite the rifle that leaned near to her hand. Old Calhoun and Jim talked in low tones.

From the cell Ramiez began to jeer again. He had slept, and awakened full of confidence again. Jim Raine's lips tightened. He rose, strode into the cell-block. He wasn't going to have Ella awakened by that jackal: she needed her rest.

He took out his gun as he halted outside the cell door. He said:

'If you don't shut your face *señor* skunk I'll come in there an' beat you over the head . . . '

'I'll see that you die long and hard, young pup!'

'One more word!'

But Don Ramiez shut up. This young gringo meant what he said. He was a real lobo and his fangs were sharp and white. The Don didn't want to be laid senseless on the dirty floor of the cell. This would demean him before Ponch Bates who was little more than a peon, though he was Ben Jagar's right-hand man. Ramiez needed Ponch; for he needed Jagar. He went to the back of the cell and sat down on the bunk beside Ponch and ignored the young gringo now.

Jim went back into the office. Ella was still sleeping peacefully. Her father was rolling himself a cigarette. He tossed the makings over to Jim. They made themselves smokes, lit up.

Although Jim had been wary of this old turkey-cock when they first met, they were good friends now. Old Calhoun was a man after his own heart who took no sass from nobody. He found himself telling the oldster all about the KP, about his father, about Curly and the tragedy.

Old Calhoun was sympathetic. He realized the burning desire for justice and revenge that was riding this younker. He liked Jim. Jim reminded him of himself as a younker; he had been full of fire all the time too. He chuckled to himself; he didn't mind admitting that he was still somewhat of an old rooster. He was looking forward to the coming fight. He had been stuck behind a store counter too long.

Ella yawned prettily and stretched. She was a slim clean-limbed young female with everything in the right place and beautifully so. She awoke. At the same time Rabby and Nevada entered and said Sal was waiting back at the lodging house with breakfast.

Old Calhoun grinned at his daughter. 'Yuh certainly woke up just right, honey. Hungry?'

'I sure am.'

Ella smiled at Jim. He grinned. The very look of this girl warmed him, dissipated some of his tensions. He escorted her down the street. Old

Calhoun, his two Colts tucked into his belt, brought up the rear.

The town looked pretty much the same as usual. But there was a tension in the air, a brooding stillness that was not wholly brought about by the hot sun. There was not so much chatter and noise of work and business going on. People did not yell greetings to each other. They even eyed each other doubtfully as if they were in the midst of potential enemies. Everybody wore a gun. The town bristled with weapons. Even the people who had scoffed at the thought of attack had not been courageous and sure enough of their convictions to leave their weapons at home. There was an apprehensive quietness.

Before turning into Sal's yard, the three people looked towards the bluff where one of the guards were posted. He saw them looking and waved and they waved back. His wave had been nonchalant. Evidently he could not see anything to worry him.

Over breakfast, big Sal said: 'I had some bad news this morning.'

'What was that?' asked Ella.

'You remember old Mrs. Crocket I used to sit up with o' nights sometimes.'

'Yes.'

Jim looked from one to the other of the two women then back again. Sal said:

'She died at four o'clock this morning . . . '

'Oh, what a shame. The poor old dear.'

'Well, it's been expected of course. She's very old. Her hubby's been dead longer than I care to remember. But I shall miss the old lady. She and her man were among the first settlers in this part of the country. They had to fight Injuns as well as folks like Don Ramiez an' his hell's brood. All her children went back East. She'd got nobody left except me an' a few others who used to go an' sit with her o' nights. My, that old besom could tell some tales of the old days . . . '

A look almost of tenderness came over Sal's hardbitten face under its crowning glory. This big woman had so many facets to her character; Jim Raine thought he could see tears glistening in her fine green eyes.

Consequently, he was somewhat startled when she whirled suddenly and fixed those bright eyes on him — on him alone — in a basilisk stare.

'I don't think you believed me, did you, young James, when I told you about my sick friend?'

Jim's mouth opened and closed wordlessly a couple of times. Then he decided to make a clean breast of it. You couldn't fool an old stager like Sal. He said:

'I wasn't sure. I had to keep an open mind. I didn't know yuh then, y'know . . . '

'Is that why you busted my door open that night? Did you expect to find me hiding under the bed?'

Jim gaped. Ella gave a little ripple of laughter. Old Calhoun chuckled and wheezed. Jim's lean brown young face slowly creased into a grin. It was the kind of grin that would have charmed any woman and Sal's simulated wrath was not proof against it. She grinned too. Then she began to laugh, deep-throated, her big, comely body shaking. She threw back her head and her laughter peeled louder.

Soon they were all laughing fit to burst. All thoughts of an impending attack, of killing, of justice and vengeance were washed from their minds. Jim laughed till his ribs ached. He saw Ella on the other side of the table with tears streaming down her cheeks. He thought she looked more charming than ever. He had an inkling of what life could be like with a woman like this sitting across the table from him every morning. A ranch — a man's work — a good woman . . .

She saw him watching her and slowly

she became still. But there was something in her dark eyes, still washed bright with laughter, that called to his. He turned his gaze away first. They had all stopped laughing now and sat in weak attitudes. He looked at Sal and said:

'I'll fix that door right now if you'll find me some tools.'

'The tools are in the big whatnot on the landing. Show him, Ella, will you?'

'Yes,' said the girl softly and led the way.

Behind the backs of the two young people Sal winked broadly at old Calhoun. All he could do was chuckle weakly again, almost soundlessly. The footsteps of the two young people died on the stairs.

Ella got the toolbox out of the 'whatnot' and Jim carried it along to the door of Sal's room. Neither of them said anything. She followed him and when they reached the door he handed the box back to her and she held it while he inspected the lock. He had a man's seriousness over the job and she was content to hand his tools to him as he needed them. This trivial little job seemed to bring them closer together.

They spoke now, but only in monosyllables. There was an understanding between them now. They both sensed it. It needed no words to explain it.

The job was soon done. But they kept trying the door, seriously, with grave faces. It was as if they were reluctant to break the bond it had given them. But they moved along the passage again finally and still the bond remained unbroken. It was still there, subtle, but there. And they both knew now that it was too strong to break. It had been forged by little things — laughter over a breakfast table, a small job well done together — rather than the bloody adventure in which they found themselves. But the strife and hate would go and there would still be the little things with which to build a life together; the little things and the enduring things.

Ella took the toolbox from Jim once more and put it back into the 'whatnot'. As she rose again, her dark eyes looked into his and he bent and kissed her. Their arms went around each other easily, stayed there as if they belonged.

And after a time the girl drew herself gently free and said, 'We better go down now, Jim.'

And he said, 'All right, *chiquita*.'

That was what her father used to call her mother, she remembered. There was a rightness there too.

They tried to act normally when they got back into the kitchen. And, as far as they knew, they succeeded. But Ella's father and Big Sal were much older hands at masking their feelings than the two young folks were and, if they exchanged quick, meaningful glances they took care that Ella and Jim did not intercept them.

In a little while Ella, her father, and Jim set out again while Sal stayed to do a few chores before joining them again.

Old Calhoun said: 'Would you two young critturs like to pay a visit to the guards both ends of town an' see how they're getting on. My ol' legs don't hanker for climbing like they used to.'

With studied indifference Ella and Jim said 'All right'. They set off. Old Calhoun grinned as he watched them go. He noted how they kept studiously apart. Who did they think they were fooling?

Ah, well, he wouldn't mind having young Jim for a son-in-law. The younker was obviously terribly smitten with Ella. And he was an honourable man. And of good stock. Landowners no less. But so was Ella of good stock. Her mother had been high-born and Calhoun himself was no pinwheel. He might be only a storekeeper right now but he was far from being a pauper. Was he going too fast he wondered? Was he going too fast because he didn't want his daughter to stay in this godforsaken neck of the woods any longer?

No, he didn't think so! They had reached the guard up there and he had risen to greet them. They were much closer together now.

15

The look-out guards had nothing to report. They had seen nothing out there on the sun-hazed plain. They were beginning to think they would never see anything, that nothing would happen after all. Jim said the guard would have to be trebled by night and left with something to think about.

Twilight came. The day's work was done. Jim, Rabby, Nevada, old Calhoun and Sal began to push things again. The townsfolk might be trying to kid themselves that the raiders would not come after all. But these five people and, it may be said, the erstwhile vigilantes who accompanied them, did not try to kid themselves. They were still sure the raiders would come. They made the rounds. They finally got people on building barricades at each end of the main drag. By this time it was full dark.

Carts were dragged to block the street, were ballasted by barrels and chests. Horse-troughs were emptied of water and upturned. They made pretty effective bulwarks. Vantage points were chosen at upstairs windows and on the few outside balconies. There was no means of knowing from which side the raiders would attack. They might come from both sides. Some people said a small party might come in by stealth and try to get the Don out of jail. If this happened the town and its elaborate precautions would look pretty silly.

On the other hand, if the raiders came in force there was a big possibility that the townsfolk would be considerably outnumbered. Many of them were not fighters; they were indifferent shots. But enthusiasm had seized them now and they bragged of what they would do when the raiders came. They'd show 'em! Old enmities were forgotten. The people were drawn together by a common purpose. They began to look upon this thing as a great adventure. Rabby Buckthorne said cynically that he hoped they wouldn't change their tune when the raiders did come, that they wouldn't scatter like sheep. Nevada said that if people had to fight they'd fight. Jim said both of them had been around horses and mules too long; why didn't they just wait and see? He left them then. It was his turn on guard.

He picked up the two men who were to accompany him. They were younkers like himself, men especially picked for this more hazardous night duty. And the guard had, as Jim had suggested earlier, been trebled. Three other men were at this moment making their way to the look-out at the other end of town to relieve the single guard there.

Jim and his two partners had the guard looking out towards the Cracker-jacks. It was from this direction that the raiders were most likely to come, unless they made a wide detour when they left the Ramiez rancho. There was a rise, a cluster of boulders that made a fair cover. The single guard rose from among these and stretched himself.

'I'm suttinly glad you boys have come. I was getting to the stage of talking to myself. I haven't seen a thing. Not that you can see a thing now. But I haven't heard a thing either . . . '

'Yeh, it's purty dark,' said Jim curtly. 'We mustn't let the skunks crawl up on us. They'll hear us a mile off if we yap too loud.'

'Yeh, sure, I didn't think of that,' whispered the garrulous guard as Jim ushered him on his way.

Jim's two pards were Mort and Lafe respectively. Mort was a surly taciturn character. There was little danger of his talking too loud. Lafe seemed an intelligent cuss. He spoke in whispers. Neither of them were fighting men as Jim, brought up in the hard life of a ranch, was a fighting man. They were sons of storekeepers who, like their fathers, had turned blind eyes to the lack of law in Pinto Gap, the things that went on there. Being storekeepers and necessary they had not been molested. Perhaps no blame could be attached to them for going along as they had. Jim hoped they had been aroused enough now to be able to give an account of themselves when the time came. He tried not to show the contempt he felt for them. He loved fighting and he didn't mind admitting this. His blood sang in anticipation of the fray to come.

These two bozos had keen eyes and ears: that was what they had been picked for. They were, at least, the best of an indifferent bunch.

The night was black. Last night and the night before there had been brilliant moonlight. But now even the forces of nature seemed to be ranging themselves on the side of evil. The wind soughed morbidly, scattering dust and leaves, bringing little unnamed sounds, making men start and grip their weapons, straining their eyes and ears in the blackness. A coyote yelped off in the hills. The horses belonging to the three look-outs stirred uneasily. Jim had thought it wise to bring their mounts in case they had to make a quick retreat back into town. Rabby Buckthorne, ex-Indian fighter, had taught his protégé well.

Lafe whispered, 'Do you think they'll come tonight?'

Jim said, 'It's early yet. They'll probably wait until they think we're drowsy.'

But in this he was wrong. They heard the hammering of the hooves from afar. A big force of men and horses, the sound rolling like thunder, coming steadily nearer.

Mort, the taciturn one, cursed under his breath. Jim said, 'Three of us certainly can't hold that mob off. Let's get the horses.'

They mounted up. 'Wait till we can see them,' said Jim. 'Then give them all you've got an' turn an' get back to town.'

'I'm not waiting for that mob,' yelled

Mort. 'I'm riding back to give the alarm.'

Next moment he had turned his horse and was riding into the night. Jim went as if to go after him, then changed his mind.

'He always was a yellow-belly,' said Lafe.

Jim said, 'Well, there's only two of us now. You want to leave?'

'I'll stick if you will.'

'Right. Here they come!'

* * *

'Now!' screamed Jim.

He squeezed the trigger of his repeating rifle again and again. Horses and riders loomed up in front of him, faded in dust and smoke and noise.

He shoved his hot and empty rifle into his saddle-boot and automatically drew his two guns, one his own, the other one he had borrowed. He was vaguely aware of Lafe triggering beside him. He was blinded and deafened by dust and smoke and the acrid smell of gunpowder. His horse pitched and tossed like a boat in a gale. He held on desperately with his knees.

The attackers, taken by surprise in the blackness, had broken into two separate bunches. A horse threshed on the ground. A man was pinned beneath the beast and, in the lull between the firing he could be heard crying out in a high-pitched wail over and over again. Another man lay prone near him. He had been hit; his horse had probably bolted.

Lafe and Jim had no means of knowing how many more of the raiders they had hit. They glanced at each other, both of them very relieved to see that his companion was unhurt. But already slugs were coming perilously close again and the raiders were coming on in a pincer movement calculated to cut the two men off; and after that they wouldn't stand a hoot in hell.

'Let's get out of here!' screamed Jim.

Lafe nodded. They wheeled their

horses. They fired all the time. They were firing over their shoulders as they sped away. The raiders had been a little demoralised at meeting opposition earlier than they had expected. But they must have realized by now that there were only two men; they sped after them like fiends right out of hell.

'Round the back here!' yelled Jim. 'Rabby an' Nevada will be expecting us. If we go straight on we're liable to be cut down by some of our own men.'

Lafe knew this but Jim had figured he ought to remind him anyway. He wasn't sure whether Lafe could hear him. Involuntarily, he looked over his shoulder.

Lafe's horse was still galloping all out, his mane streaming in the wind. But Lafe was no longer in the saddle. He had been hit and had fallen. His heel had caught in the stirrup and he was being dragged along by the frantic horse, terrified by the lightness of the saddle and yet this strange dragging thing that he could not seem to shake off, more terrified of this than he had been by all the shooting and the smoke and the dust.

Jim's horrified pause had given Lafe's horse chance to catch up and now the two beasts ran neck and neck. Lafe's body bumped along like a dummy. Jim knew there was nothing he could do for this new-found pard of his; now lost so quickly and terribly. A gust of rage shook him. Lafe had stayed. Lafe who was not a fighting-man: he had known the odds and he had stayed. The other one had run yelping with his tail between his legs, like a yellow cur. But Lafe had stayed and look what had happened to him!

The main bunch of raiders were making for the main drag. Four of them had veered off and kept after Jim. Rabby and Nevada stepped out of cover, yelling at Jim as he went past.

The two old-timers opened up. Three of the men were fetched from their saddles. The other one turned tail and bolted. Jim had reined in at the back of the jail. As Rabby and Nevada caught him up he was gently extricating Lafe's foot from the stirrup.

Lafe had stopped a bullet in the back of the head. His young face was not good to look upon. They carried him into the passage beside the cell-block and covered him with a blanket and left him there. From the cell Pablo Ramiez called:

'One of your pigeons down already, huh, *amigos*? But it will come to all of you.' He began to laugh, a high cackle, and Ponch Bates joined sycophantically in with him.

Rabby Buckthorne took the bunch of keys from the hook in the passage. With his gun in his other hand he crossed to the cell door. He opened the cell door.

Ramiez was still cackling when Rabby hit him across the side of the head with the barrel of the gun. The noise died with a gurgle and the noble Don slumped unconscious to the floor. Like a cornered rat, Ponch Bates leapt at Rabby. Jim and Nevada started forward. But Rabby did not need any help. He twisted, whirled. The gun rose and fell again. Ponch fell on top of his cell-mate.

Rabby locked them in again. 'That'll keep 'em quiet for a while I guess. They've been on like that ever since you left, Jim. When they heard the shooting I thought Ramiez was going crazy with joy the way he shrieked.'

'He *is* crazy,' said Nevada. 'Maybe you ought to have shot both of them then like the mad dogs they are.'

There didn't seem any answer to this; Nevada went on, 'What happened to that other younker who went out with you, Jim? Mort something — whatever his name was.'

Jim told them about Mort. Their silence was eloquent as they went on into the office. Ella's face lit up when she saw Jim. But she did not run forward. She knew he was needed at the barricades. Brodie, the blacksmith, and the rest of the 'vigilantes' were already there, and so was Big Sal. Old Calhoun and his daughter had stayed behind to watch the prisoners while Rabby and Nevada went to pick up Jim.

Old Calhoun wanted to get in on the fighting outside, but there was no time to argue: he agreed to stay in the office, watching the back while the three partners helped out outside. Ella, of course, stayed with her father. Calhoun said she was a better shot than he was anyway.

Jim pressed Ella's hand quickly before he went. Neither of them said anything. She was a staunch young frontiers woman; she knew what was before them. Her heart went with him to strengthen him in the fight.

The raiders had only come in at one end of town. The townsfolk, forewarned by the firing from the lookout point, met them with a blistering hail of lead from behind the barricades, from windows and balconies.

The people of Pinto Gap were reborn that night. Some of them died so that others might have a new life. The town as a whole became a new town, a town in which its people could take pride, a town worth fighting for. The townsfolk fought because they had to fight, but through the blood and death and travail they were rejuvenated. They had great examples before them; they would not easily forget the young cowboy with the lean dark face, the one called Jim, who was a fighting man par excellence, a figure in a smoke-wreathed Western legend. They would not easily forget his two partners either, the two wrinkled men as old as time itself. They fought together like a well-oiled machine, uttering their shrill Injun-fighter whoops all the time, grinning at each other like a couple of mischievous devils from hell . . .

The raiders fell back. Then came on again. But they could not breech the defences. They left their dead behind them on the dusty cart-rutted street. There were lights here and it was noted that the raiders were led by Ben Jagar, who seemed to bear a charmed life.

He was a big mis-shapen man on a big horse. He kept waving his men on and they obeyed him as if he was God Himself. The Ramiez peons obeyed him too: had they not sought his aid to raze this town to the ground and rescue their chief from a gringo hang-rope? The young Mexican who had fooled Jim Raine and escaped was well in the forefront of the attacking waves until a bullet in the brain laid him low forever.

Turning at the barricade, Jim Raine came face to face with the cowardly Mort.

Mort said: 'Where's Lafe?'

Jim swung his fist round in a back-handed blow which caught Mort full in the mouth and knocked him sprawling. Jim bent momentarily over him. 'You speak to me again an' I'll kill yuh,' he said.

Mort just lay there, half-petrified with fright. Turning away from him, Jim saw Ben Jagar on the other side of the barricade. There was no mistaking that hump-backed, big-bellied figure. Jim's killing rage was turned on the man who had murdered his brother. He shot at Jagar, but again the big man's luck held and the slug only took his hat off. The horse pranced, whirling. Jim tried to get set for another shot but somebody else beat him to it. This time the slug hit the horse. The beast squealed shrilly and went down. Jagar was thrown clear.

Jagar scrambled to his feet, limping a little. Before anybody could stop him, Jim Raine had leapt over the barricade.

'Cover him,' yelled Rabby Buck-thorne. 'Shoot carefully.'

Ben Jagar saw Jim approaching and reached for his gun in the dust. He raised it swiftly, his lips curling back from strong yellow teeth.

Jim shot him three times in the chest. Ben's only shot jerked a fragment of cloth from the cowboy's shoulder. Ben's wolfish grin turned to a fixed and horrible grimace. His eyes mirrored terrible surprise before the light faded from them. He pitched forward in the dust and his gun fell before him, his fingers still clawed in death a few inches from the notched walnut butt.

Rabby had gotten over the barricade too by now. He dragged Jim into cover by main force. The younker looked as if he wanted to fight the rest of the bunch on his lonesome. But he came to his senses. 'Thanks, pardner,' he said.

He looked at the shapeless bundle in the street. That had been his enemy!

He was empty now.

No more hate. No more frustration. No more tension . . .

The raiders were demoralised by the death of their leader, by the simple and terrible way it had happened. Those that survived, turned and fled.

Ella met Jim at the doorway of the jail. Again they did not say anything. He enfolded her in his arms. Rabby and Nevada grinned at each other, swerving around the locked couple carefully in order to enter the office.

'So it's all over,' said old Calhoun.

He was kind of disgruntled because nobody had tried to storm the jail.

'I guess Ramiez and his pard have woken up,' he went on. 'I heard 'em cursing I thought a mite ago. I'll go in an' tell 'em the glad news. The circuit judge should be here in a couple o' days. Those two skunks are as good as swinging right now.'

Rabby said: 'We wouldn't want 'em at the wedding anyway.'

He raised his voice on the last few words but there was no sound from the shadows beyond the doorway.

THE END

We do hope that you have enjoyed reading this large print book.

Did you know that all of our titles are available for purchase?

We publish a wide range of high quality large print books including:
Romances, Mysteries, Classics
General Fiction
Non Fiction and Westerns

Special interest titles available in large print are:
The Little Oxford Dictionary
Music Book, Song Book
Hymn Book, Service Book

Also available from us courtesy of Oxford University Press:
Young Readers' Dictionary
(large print edition)
Young Readers' Thesaurus
(large print edition)

For further information or a free brochure, please contact us at:
Ulverscroft Large Print Books Ltd.,
The Green, Bradgate Road, Anstey,
Leicester, LE7 7FU, England.
Tel: (00 44) 0116 236 4325
Fax: (00 44) 0116 234 0205

STONE MOUNTAIN

Concho Bradley

The stage robbery had been accomplished by an old woman. Twine Fourch had never heard of a female being a highway robber before. He followed the trail all the way to a dilapidated log cabin up Stone Mountain. What happened after that no one could believe even after townsmen from Jefferson found the old log house and the skeletal dying old woman. But before the mystery could be solved there would be two unnecessary killings, a bizarre suicide and a lynching.

GUNS OF THE GAMBLER

M. Duggan

Destitute gambler Ben Crow arrives in Mallory keen to claim his inheritance, only to discover that rancher Edward Bacon has other ideas. Set up by Miss Dorothy, who had fooled him completely, Ben finds himself dangling on the end of a rope. Saved from death, Ben sets off in pursuit of Miss Dorothy, determined upon retribution. However, his quest for vengeance turns into a rescue mission when she is kidnapped by a crazy man-burning bandit.

SIDEWINDER

John Dyson

All Flynn wants is to be Marshal of Tucson, but he is framed by the territory's richest rancher, Frank Buchanan, and thrown into Yuma prison. Five years later Flynn comes out, intent on clearing his name and burning for vengeance. Fists thud, knives flash and bullets fly as he rides both sides of the law and participates in kidnapping and double-dealing. He is once again arrested for a murder of which he is innocent. Can he escape the noose a second time?